What the reviewers said about *The Mysterious Naiad:*

"Mystery, whimsy, humor, romance, nostalgia and more
in one . . . larger than usual Naiad offering . . . this one
will take you through a week at the beach or the cabin,
or it will be welcome on the nightstand for quite a while."

Alabama FORUM

"Stories in this collection covered the entire spectrum of
intrigue and entertainment. A few were . . . quite bizarre.
All in all *The Mysterious Naiad* is a fantastic book for
late night reading."

Jean Rosalia
Queereview

"Another wonderful collection of short stories by the ever
growing house of Naiad authors . . . The only problem I
see with these wonderful collections of Naiad authors is
that at some point they may run out of genres or stories."

Jane Addams Books

"A good short story is better than practically anything.
Naiad's latest collection of short works by its authors, a
group of writers that get more impressive each year, is
very fine indeed."

Deborah Peifer
Bay Area Reporter

"*The Mysterious Naiad* . . . another in the successful line
of Naiad romance anthologies — this time the stable of
mystery writers pen the steamy scenes."

Marie Kuda
Outlines

THE FIRST TIME EVER

Love Stories by Naiad Press Authors

EDITED BY

BARBARA GRIER AND **CHRISTINE CASSIDY**

THE FIRST TIME EVER

Love Stories by Naiad Press Authors

EDITED BY

BARBARA GRIER AND **CHRISTINE CASSIDY**

THE NAIAD PRESS, INC.

1997

Printed in the United States of America on acid-free paper
First Edition
Second Printing April 1997

Cover designer: Bonnie Liss (Phoenix Graphics)
Typesetter: Sandi Stancil

Library of Congress Cataloging-in-Publication Data

The first time ever : love stories by Naiad Press authors / edited by Barbara Grier and Christine Cassidy
   p.   cm.
   ISBN 1-56280-086-8 (pbk.)
   1. Lesbians—Fiction. 2. Love stories, American—Women authors. 3. Lesbians' writings, American. 4. First loves—Fiction. I. Grier, Barbara, 1933 – . II. Cassidy, Christine.
PS648 .L47F57   1995
813'.085089287—dc20   95-14531
                           CIP

ABOUT THE EDITORS

Barbara Grier

Author, editor, bibliographer, writings include *The Lesbian in Literature, Lesbiana, The Lesbian's Home Journal, Lavender Herring, Lesbian Lives* as well as contributions to various anthologies, *The Lesbian Path* (Cruikshank) and *The Coming Out Stories* (Stanley and Wolfe). She is co-editor, with Katherine V. Forrest, of *The Erotic Naiad* (1992), *The Romantic Naiad* (1993) and *The Mysterious Naiad* (1994).

Her early career included working for sixteen years with the pioneer lesbian magazine *The Ladder*. For the last twenty-three years she has been, together with Donna J. McBride, the guiding force behind THE NAIAD PRESS.

Articles about Barbara's and Donna's life are too numerous to list, but a good early overview can be found in *Heartwoman* by Sandy Boucher (N.Y., Harper, 1982).

She lives in Tallahassee, Florida.

Christine Cassidy

Christine Cassidy is the Director of Marketing and Circulation at Poets & Writers, Inc., a contributing editor to the *Lambda Book Report* and an editor for the Naiad Press since 1988. A poet, she is the recipient of a New Jersey State Council on the Arts grant in poetry. She also writes reviews, essays, articles and stories, and has been published in *The Persistent Desire: A Femme/Butch Reader, The Lambda Book Report, Our World, Poets & Writers Magazine,* and *On Our Backs,* among others. She can be seen, courtesy of photographer Morgan Gwenwald, in *Butch/Femme,* a lively collection of photos edited by MG Soares. She lives in New York City.

TABLE OF CONTENTS

Not Me
Claire McNab

"More!"

Raw sensation blacked out my thoughts. I was rising, breathless, pulsating with a relentless rhythm. I spread my legs, rose up to her mouth, pitched like a boat in a storm.

"Yes!"

She raised her head, pleased with herself. "Pretty good, eh?"

"The best."

She wormed her way up my body until she lay

beside me. I absently stroked her hair. What was her name? Rosalyn? Rosalie?

"I'd like to see you again, Lois," she said against my neck. At least *she* had a memory for names.

"I'd like that too, but I'm going to be away next weekend, and . . ."

She laughed softly. "And thanks, but no thanks?"

I was relieved at her undemanding amusement. "Well, maybe. But it's been great."

"Yes, it has," she said with feeling. "You're just terrific in bed."

I tightened my arm about her. She was pretty damn good herself.

I avoided suggesting we spend the rest of the day together. As we dressed she looked across the crumpled bed at me. Tucking her shirt into her black jeans, she said, "See you around, maybe at Harpy's . . ."

Harpy's was the bar where we'd picked each other up in an unspoken contract for one night of mutual pleasure. I said enthusiastically, "I look forward to it."

Jeez, I thought, *we always say the same things, me and anyone I bring home. And we always mean . . . what? It's been nice, but . . . ?*

I wondered what it would be like to have the same person in bed with me night after night. Of course, I'd tried that once, years ago it seemed, and it had ultimately been a disaster. Looking back, I couldn't decide why I'd agreed to live with Jean. Perhaps it had seemed to be the thing to do at the time, but I certainly hadn't loved her. *Love* — that dumb word that everyone used so freely. I knew what love was, of course. I loved women in general, I loved my parents, I loved animals, I loved rum and raisin ice cream. No one could fairly accuse me of being without emotions.

Sunday morning, alone. Suddenly feeling depressed, I wished I had a dog to walk in the park, or put in the car and take for a ride. Living in rented places meant no pets because I couldn't bear the idea of keeping a cat or a dog confined. One day, I was always promising myself, I'd buy a house with a big back yard, and have two huge dogs and five cats for company.

The day stretched empty ahead of me. I called my best friend, Ruby, and caught her on her way out. "Picnic," she said. "It's a nice woman. You haven't met her yet." Ruby had only just started dating again. After the breakup twelve months ago of her ten-year partnership she'd been so upset I'd felt relieved that *I* didn't have anyone in my life who could hurt me that way.

I tried a few other friends and got their answering machines. I knew I'd get my parents at home, so I did a duty call, which took up half an hour or so. Now what? I snatched up the phone when it rang, then sank back disappointed. It was my boss. "Lois? I hate to ask you for a favor, but I'm in a bind."

"Not me, Maurie," I said. Maurie Shore was okay to work for, but our department of Worldwide Freight Services had just finished the long grind of doing a full presentation to upper management of our direction and goals for the next three years, and I was tired of work and everything to do with it.

Maurie sounded harassed. "Lois, I wouldn't ask if there was anyone else I could get. I know how hard you've been working, but there's a computer consultant coming in from Melbourne on a one o'clock flight today, and someone has to meet her, because I can't."

"Why can't you?" I was damned if I was going to volunteer for anything to do with work.

"Fact is," said Maurie, "June's just gone into premature labor, weeks early, and I need to be with her."

I'd met Maurie's wife once at an office party, but could only remember an unremarkable woman with a sort of hazy niceness about her. "Who is it and what flight?" I asked, resigned to being cooperative.

His relief obvious, he reeled off the details. ". . . And I'd really appreciate it, Lois, if you could look after her for the rest of the day. I did promise to show her around Sydney this afternoon . . ."

I managed not to groan aloud. Sure, I'd been feeling lonely, but that didn't mean I welcomed the idea of being charming to some woman who was probably only interested in software and computer chips, or, worse still, had interminable stories about her husband and children.

Of course the plane was late. I was really irritated by the time the passengers started to stream out of the gate. Since Maurie had had no idea what she looked like, I had lettered a large card with her name, DAWN LOGAN, and stood like an idiot holding it at breast height. My hopes rose when an extremely attractive redhead examined the card as she walked toward me, but she swept by and I was left surveying her retreating back.

"I'm Dawn Logan," said a low voice, "but you can't be Maurie Shore."

I thought for a moment we'd met before, but realized it was because she was the most relentlessly average person I'd ever seen — average height, average weight, average looks. Naturally her hair was mid-brown, an indeterminate color I call Brilliant Mouse. At least *my* hair had chestnut highlights. She wore anonymous, well-cut clothes, inconspicuous jewelry — no wedding ring — and carried a tan briefcase.

We shook hands formally, and I explained why I was replacing Maurie. As we waited for the carousel to spit out her luggage, I inspected Dawn Logan out of the corner of my eye. She was older than me, and her manner was much more reserved. *Boring* was the word that came to mind. And I had to spend the rest of the day with her, unless I could dump her at her hotel and gracefully disappear.

"I haven't been in Sydney for a long time," she said. "In fact, I've only been back in Australia for a few months, after several years in the U.K." Her smile was pleasant — actually, quite beguiling.

I heard myself say, "Maurie was going to show you around the city this afternoon. I'd be happy to stand in for him."

"Would you really?" She laughed, a nice, throaty sound. "I'm sure you've got better things to do."

"No, I haven't." Dawn Logan no doubt thought I was being polite, but it was true.

I had to admit she wasn't bad company, although she didn't talk much about anything, including herself. Wondering if she might be of the sisterhood, I threw out a few oblique references, but she ignored them, so I gave a mental shrug and concentrated on being a tourist guide.

Late in the afternoon, as I drove home after dropping her at the serviced apartment the company was renting for her, I realized with chagrin that Dawn Logan knew a damn sight more about me than I did about her. That wasn't the way I liked to work — I had always aspired to being a Woman of Mystery because, frankly, I figured it made me more intriguing.

Next morning I called Ruby at work. "How was the heavy date?"

Her chuckle came down the line. "Promising. Very promising."

"And what was she like in bed?"

Ruby tut-tutted. "Please! This was our first date. And don't bother telling me what you would have done in my place."

This was an area where she'd criticized me before, so I steered the conversation around to my Sunday activities. Ruby was interested. "Do you like her?"

"I suppose so. I mean, there's not much to like, or dislike. She's just an ordinary person."

"No spark? An irresistible desire didn't sweep over you?"

I snorted, and was about to explain why this was impossible when Dawn Logan put her head around the door. "Lois? When you're free there's some stuff I'd like to go over with you."

Smiling cooperatively, I hoped she hadn't overheard me and made the connection with herself. Dawn had been introduced to everyone first thing that morning, and she was, as the management suit told us with a satisfied smirk, "going to streamline our systems to get the most out of our computer network."

Over the next few days I had a lot to do with
Dawn, and found I was warming to her. She certainly
knew her job, and she had a dry sense of humor that
was very entertaining.

Ruby called me on Saturday to ask if I'd meet
her at Harpy's that night. Plump and cheerful, she
bounced up to greet me at the entrance. Harpy's was
just warming up, and a wall of music and conversation hit us as soon as we made it down the narrow
stairs and through the swing doors. Ruby linked arms
with me. "And how are you getting on with Dawn?"

I glared at her. "What is this fixation on the
Logan woman? I just work with her, that's all. And,
as far as I know, she's straight." I turned my attention to the bar and waved to a couple of friends,
Bonnie and Lynn. We started to make our way
toward them across the crowded dance floor.

Ruby ran into me when I suddenly stopped.
"What?" she said, when her dig in the ribs didn't
move me.

"Rubes! That woman at the other end of the
bar . . . that's Dawn Logan!"

Ruby craned past me. "Which one? The butchy
number?"

"Hardly. The average looking one talking to the
woman in the yellow top."

"Introduce me," said Ruby with an enthusiastic
smile.

"No way! I have to work with her."

Ruby ignored me. She wriggled past a clump of
people and headed for Dawn. I kept my dignity,
joining our friends and wedging a hip against the
bar. I ordered a drink, trying to keep up a casual
conversation while simultaneously watching the

mirror behind the bar to see what in the hell Ruby
was doing. I saw her reach Dawn, start an animated
conversation, and gesture in my direction. Making a
silent vow to kill Ruby, I talked about nothing in
particular while covertly watching the two of them
make their way down the bar toward us.

"Hey, everyone," said Ruby. "This is Dawn. She
works with Lois."

Dawn seemed perfectly relaxed. She nodded to me,
smiled at Bonnie and Lynn, and began chatting about
the changes she'd noticed in Sydney since she'd been
away. I watched her while she talked. Sure, she was
average-looking, even plain, but she had a warmth
and vitality that was really quite attractive.

Ruby dug me in the ribs and indicated Dawn.
"And you thought she was straight," she whispered
mockingly. "Going to go for it?"

I rolled my eyes. "Are you kidding me?"

Ruby pursed her lips. "Well, if you're not
interested, *I* might be . . ."

"What happened to the nice woman you saw last
weekend?"

"Thinking of taking a leaf from your book," said
Ruby with a grin. "Playing the field, I think it's
called."

Of course Dawn was nothing to me, but I felt
subtly betrayed when Ruby monopolized her. I went
home from Harpy's early, and alone — which was
pretty unusual for me.

On Sunday Bonnie and Lynn were throwing a
lunch to show off the house they had just bought
together. I wandered into the crowded kitchen to find
Dawn Logan making a fruit punch. "Hi," she said,
friendly but not overly interested.

This wasn't good enough. I decided to spend some time charming her. Dawn was pleasant, but restrained. When she'd excused herself to take the bowl of punch into the dining room, Ruby, who'd been lounging against the kitchen bench, said, "Not interested, eh?"

"Give me time," I snapped.

Two weeks passed. Every morning at work I found myself watching for Dawn. I couldn't quite remember why I'd thought her such an average run-of-the-mill woman when we had first met. She had an easy confidence in her abilities, a keen wit, a graceful walk . . . I really liked her. A lot.

The problem was, I couldn't quite figure out what she thought about *me*. She was always friendly, but there was a reserve underneath her smile. Even so, I knew a great deal about her as a person because we had been working closely together. She was patient, intelligent, hardworking. In situations where I would have blown my top, she remained cool and in control. No one pushed her around, not even a couple of Neanderthal guys in shipping I'd had trouble with.

One Friday morning I woke up to find I'd been dreaming about her. Things were getting out of hand. Dawn was always early to work, so I made it in before most people had even left home and casually sidled up to her as she made herself a cup of coffee.

"Hi," she said, and smiled.

This was ridiculous. I felt positively nervous. "Dawn, I was wondering . . ."

"Yes?"

"I was wondering if we could have dinner sometime. Like tonight." I hoped I looked nonchalant. I didn't want her to think it was any big deal.

"Okay, let's do it."

I wasn't prepared for such an immediate response. Wasn't she going to play hard to get? When Ruby called me to check on my plans for the weekend, I was surprised to hear a smug tone in my voice. "Going out to dinner tonight," I announced. "With Dawn."

It was irritating to realize that Ruby was amused, rather than impressed. "Sure you can handle this, Lois?"

"Oh, *please!*

We had dinner in a little Italian restaurant. Too late I remembered that it was difficult, if not impossible, to eat spaghetti and look smooth. Dawn, of course, had chosen a more manageable dish. Still, I found myself enjoying the evening so much that I kept ordering cappuccino after cappuccino to stretch it out. I was awash with so much caffeine that I was undoubtedly facing serious sleep problems by the time she said, "Lois, this has been fun, but I really must go home."

My heart rose, although there was no invitation in her manner. Her apartment. And I was the one with a car, so I was driving her there. I could imagine . . .

Nothing went the way I expected. I walked her to her door, although she said it wasn't necessary. When she didn't seem inclined to ask me in, I leaned forward and kissed her. I made it my best kiss — long, lingering, sweet.

"That was nice," she said.

"Nice? Is that all?" And *I* was trying to hide the fact that I was breathless.

Dawn gave me a polite smile. "Okay. *Very* nice, then."

This wasn't satisfactory, but I could hardly say anything more on the subject, so I moved to kiss her again. She stepped back. "Thanks for your company, Lois."

My company? For a moment I actually thought she was going to shake hands with me, but she merely touched my arm, and disappeared inside. I stared at the blank surface of the door. There was a security viewer looking at me like a single eye. What if Dawn was watching me from the other side? Just in case she was, I looked bored, although I wasn't sure what I felt. Disappointment? Anger? Admiration?

Admiration? I wasn't used to being treated this way, particularly when I was making a genuine effort, but Dawn had qualities I was only beginning to appreciate. During the night — I was right about the caffeine — I went over and over the evening. I was sure she liked my company ... Hell, I was sure she liked *me*. But how much?

The next morning Ruby turned up unannounced. She helped herself to a glass of orange juice. "Okay, tell me all about it."

"Look," I snarled, "it was just a pleasant dinner. Nothing happened."

"Did you kiss?"

"What is this? The third degree?"

Ruby grinned. "Usually I don't have to pry anything out of you. You're all too ready to give me every detail."

"There *are* no details."

"So you didn't kiss her?"

I frowned, but her expression of keen interest didn't change. "All right," I conceded. "We kissed, but that was all."

"What was it like?"

Like? It had been sensational. I'd gone weak at the knees. "Okay, I guess." I shrugged to emphasize how unimportant it all was.

Ruby's grin became open laughter. "Face it, Lois, you're falling in love with her."

"Not me. Not *me*. No way!"

Ruby's delight was sickening. "Yes, *you*," she crowed. "There's always a first time for everything. Ms. Steelheart finally crumbles."

I gave a contemptuous snort, knowing that Ruby had to be wrong about what I felt for Dawn. It was warm friendship, nothing more. The fact that I thought about her ninety percent of the time was because . . . well, I wasn't sure why it was.

After Ruby had gone I eyed the phone. Dawn might call. Maybe, like me, she hadn't been able to sleep, and had thought about our kiss, and what could have happened afterward. I snatched up the receiver and punched in her number. For some reason I knew it by heart.

The sound of her voice made my heart lift, but I was casual. "Hi. I wondered if you had any plans for tonight?"

"Lois?"

I felt indignant. Didn't she know my voice the way I knew hers? "Yes. It's Lois."

"I'm sorry. I have got plans for tonight." Dawn didn't explain.

The day turned dark. "How about tomorrow?"

"Sorry . . ."

Now I wouldn't see her until Monday morning at work. The weekend stretched like a desert before me, but I was determined to fill in the time. I hadn't been to Harpy's for ages, so tonight I'd go and look over the talent.

It was a mistake. The place was crowded and noisy, and I really didn't want to talk with anyone. I sat at a table with a group of friends and made an effort to join the conversation, but all the time I knew that I really wanted to be wherever Dawn was. It was clear I was becoming obsessive about the woman, and I rationalized that it was probably because she had proved so elusive. If I ever got her into bed I'd probably lose interest. Into bed? My imagination went into overload.

I went home early, and alone.

To stop myself from brooding, I went around to Ruby's place on Sunday afternoon. "Do you want some advice?" she asked.

Suspicious because Ruby was hiding a smile, I said, "No."

"Because I think you'll blow it with Dawn if you aren't careful."

That got my attention. "Oh, yes?"

"If you're really interested in her —"

"I'm not."

She ignored my interruption. "Then you'll slow down and concentrate on becoming friends with her first."

"We *are* friends."

Ruby looked skeptical. "Like you and me, Lois?"

"Well, no, of course not." It was true. Ruby and I

had met in school, knew each other's strengths and weaknesses, and had shared good and bad times together.

Much though I hated taking advice, I thought about what Ruby had suggested. Okay, so Dawn and I would become friends, and then ... It was the "then" that was driving me crazy. Last night I'd dreamed that we had been making love. I'd awakened tingling with desire and a yearning for her so strong it was rapidly becoming an addiction.

On Monday I began what I called, in self-mockery, *the friending of Dawn.* Only a short time ago I would have laughed to see myself planning such a long-term strategy just to win someone over, but Dawn was like no one I had ever known before.

Giving up hot pursuit and relaxing into an easy, undemanding friendship was surprisingly rewarding. Over the weeks I got to know what made Dawn laugh and cry, her opinions, the music she liked, her fears and her achievements. For my part, I found myself telling her things that I didn't even share with Ruby. It wasn't that making love wasn't on my mind — my fantasies about Dawn were incendiary — but I wanted to wait until I was sure that it would just be the icing on the cake. This was a relationship from which I wanted more than I ever had before.

When Ruby realized that I was serious, she stopped her affectionate mockery. In fact, she puzzled me by becoming uncharacteristically concerned. "Lois, don't get in too deep."

"It's a bit late to warn me now," I said. "Anyway, you were the one who encouraged me."

Ruby looked somber. "I know."

There was no planning on my part the first time

Dawn and I made love. It was cold and windy, and had been raining all weekend. We went to a movie late on Sunday afternoon and then went back to Dawn's place to indulge in the forbidden calories of wet-weather comfort food. We lit the gas fire, spread a blanket in front of it and sat cross-legged like kids. Several glasses of wine filled me with a mildly fuzzy glow. Dawn was laughing about something, and without thought I leaned over and gently kissed her cheek. She turned her head until our lips met.

I couldn't stop. Her mouth opened under mine, my heart exploded, my resolve shattered. "I love you," I heard myself gasp.

She continued to kiss me as she undressed me, and I, usually so competent in this area, felt like an alarmed, but delighted virgin. Dawn was no amateur. Her hands seemed to know my body as though we had made love before. I was bursting with passion and with an overwhelming love for her. It was exquisite, knowing that the fingers in me were hers, feeling her mouth on my nipples, her full weight on my body.

I wanted to give her the gorgeous pleasure I had just experienced. Slowly, lovingly, I touched her, tasted her, exulting as she responded to me.

A night of love. I'd often said that laughingly, scornfully. Now at last I knew what it really meant.

The next morning I felt almost shy. I so wanted Dawn to feel what I felt, but I was aware that not once had she said she loved me. We were awkward together, and she seemed relieved when I said I was going home.

When I got back to my place Ruby was waiting for me. "Lois, I have to talk to you."

"Not now, Rubes." I wanted to be alone to think about last night.

"Yes, *now*. It's important." She followed me into the kitchen. "It's about Dawn."

I grinned at her. "Last night —"

"You've never realized that you knew Dawn before, have you?"

"What?"

Ruby perched on a kitchen stool and put her elbows on the bench. "Years ago, just after you left school, you had one of your usual wham-bang affairs with her. Then, as usual, you went on to someone else. *Now* do you remember?"

I stared at her stupidly. With a jolt I remembered the moment of familiarity I'd felt when first meeting Dawn at the airport. "I couldn't have forgotten. It just isn't possible."

Ruby smiled grimly. "Given the number of short-term lovers you've had over the years, it's very possible. And she called herself Susie then. It was only later that she switched to her middle name of Dawn."

My mouth was dry. "How do you know all this?"

Ruby was flushed. "I'm sorry I ever got mixed up in this," she said ruefully. "When I saw Dawn at Harpy's I knew we'd met before. She told me who she was and asked me to keep it quiet, since you hadn't recognized her."

"But why?"

"Dawn said she fell in love with you all those years ago, but you didn't notice, or perhaps didn't care. When you went on to the next woman, she tried to forget you and got on with her life, never thinking she'd see you again. Then suddenly, she meets you again. And you don't remember her at all."

I stared at her, feeling sick. "The two of you set me up?"

Ruby nodded miserably. "Something like that."

I didn't say anything, just slammed the door as I ran out to my car.

"Ruby told me."

Dawn looked at me gravely. "I know. After you left I called her and asked her to."

I felt tears sting my eyes. "I can't believe you don't love me," I said. "Not after last night."

She looked at me steadily. "You hurt me so much. I wanted to teach you a lesson."

"Consider it taught."

Dawn put her arms around me. "Frankly," she said, "I don't think I ever quite got over you, and now I find that I absolutely adore you. However, I'll understand if you want out, after what I've done to you."

I smiled at her through my tears. "Want out?" I said. "Not me. I'm in for the long haul."

Hippie Honeymoon

Carol Schmidt

"Look, David, there're those two hitchhikers we keep running into. Kelly Hibbard and Jack-what's-his-face. Stop, stop." Lorraine Novak swept her too-long ash brown pageboy out of her face and longed once more for a good haircut, or even a warm shampoo. She felt dirty already.

That last bath in a silty glacier stream, the sun pounding at eighty degrees on her head while the water ran between her thighs at thirty-three, had about done her in on Alaska. David was having the greatest of times; she'd had enough. Ten thousand miles in four months for the simple trip from Detroit to Berkeley was too much.

David had kept saying, "We'll never be closer," when they made their first detour — northeast to Quebec, for god's sake! He'd always wanted to see Quebec. Then in Saskatchewan, when they should have been dipping south from the Trans-Canada Highway, he'd announced that they'd never be closer to Alaska, and he'd always wanted to see Alaska.

"Come on, honey, what's a few more thousand miles? When will we ever be able to do this kind of trip again? It will be something to talk about the rest of our lives."

He joked sometimes, usually while smoking a joint, about their being on a quest for the eternal meaning of life, but she suspected that it wasn't a joke for him, that he thought it was what they were really doing. Most of the time she felt as if the meaning of life might be found in a warm bath.

And she was beginning to suspect that there was nothing actually spiritual for him in this journey, only an immature boy attempting to delay the responsibilities of daily life — a thought which made her feel very old — while she was the one who was supposed to budget the money to make it all possible. So she'd kept juggling their few remaining dollars and recalculating what it would cost to get settled in Berkeley. If they ever got there.

"Thanks for stopping — we can't get through at the border!" Kelly announced. She whipped off her heather plaid English golfer's cap and let her heavy black braid tumble free; the turquoise and silver clip on the braid's end made a "plunk" sound when it hit a rivet on the back hip pocket of her Levi's.

She clambered through the side door of the J.L. Hudson's department store delivery van that David had converted into their home on wheels. Her traveling companion followed, the van's springs groaning with the extra load of two tall adults and their backpacks.

Everything Lorraine still owned was crammed into the six-foot space under the bed on which Kelly and Jack now sprawled. David had assured Lorraine that everything in her co-op apartment other than furniture would fit, even her typewriter and a kitchen-full of small appliances and too many books, though she'd had a yard sale anyway to raise a little more cash for the trip. By now she could hardly remember what she had packed and why.

He hadn't brought much at all, just two pairs of jeans and assorted tees and sweatshirts and one heavy jacket plus accompanying underwear. She was so sick of jeans and tees; laundry was costly, and the pair she had on could stand on their own. She'd priced new Levi's in Fairbanks; a pair that would have been seven dollars in Detroit was fourteen! She almost yearned to dig out the few dresses, skirts, and blouses she'd packed for work in Berkeley.

Together David and Lorraine had painted peace signs all over the forest green van; the yellow paint was now fading, and some of the peace signs looked like Mercedes emblems, others like Lawrence Welk bubbles or tipsy *e*'s. Alkan Highway dirt was an inch thick on the vehicle anyway.

As Kelly talked on in her nonstop way, Lorraine's

round face gleamed at the change in routine. She was thrilled by female companionship again. The second oldest of six kids, she'd lived alone for five years until she met her husband-to-be at an ACLU meeting. She admitted only to herself that she was suffering from too much togetherness, she and her new husband locked together for two months in a step van that sometimes felt like a cell. Today was visitors' day at the jail.

Jack she could take or leave, but Kelly was fun. She reminded Lorraine of someone in her past, she couldn't remember who. Just a happy tanned face that had looked straight at Lorraine, really looked at her, exactly the way Kelly did. For some reason she shivered.

"You can't get through the border?" she echoed Kelly's words, searching the woman's lean, angular face and heavy-fringed dark eyes. She wished once more for her packed-away eye makeup that could turn her own brown eyes into something more than pale ciphers, though she doubted Kelly ever used any.

"Yeah, the Canadian government just announced that it won't let any foreigners across its borders unless they have at least three hundred dollars in cash or a vehicle or some other kind of assets." Kelly shook her head back, letting her lustrous black braid swing free.

"Just because so many hippies came to Valdez looking for pipeline jobs and now there won't be any pipeline for another couple years, maybe not until 1973!" Jack shook his head; his wispy beard, which drifted as far below his shoulders as his sparse gray-blond hair, lay in separated strands across the front of his blue work shirt. His voice as usual had a whine to it. What ever did Kelly see in him? Once she'd caught Kelly staring at David as if to ask the same thing.

"There must be a couple dozen of us hanging around Tok, trying to figure a way out," Kelly continued. You guys won't have any trouble with this great van. It must be worth four or five hundred, easy. They'll let you through. I don't know what we're going to do, though."

"Hey, we'll sneak through the underbrush, like Rod's doing." Jack put a finger over his lips as if announcing a secret: "One of our friends headed out a couple of days ago to make a wide berth around customs by going through the wilderness."

"He'll probably be eaten by a grizzly," Lorraine said, laughing at Jack's obvious admiration for the feat.

"Naw, he'll be okay," Jack said, glancing at Kelly. "Say, do you guys have anything to eat?" Kelly punched him in the shoulder, but he continued anyway. "We were trying to put together three hundred dollars but we came up short. Kelly called her sister in Sausalito collect, and she's trying to round up some money for us, just a loan, till we get through the border."

"I told you, I don't think she'll be able to do it," Kelly said. "Her husband keeps her on a pretty tight leash. Just like you." Kelly looked pointedly at Lorraine, who quietly began preparing tuna fish sandwiches for four.

"Hey, Lorraine's free as a bird, aren't you, honey? Tell them, you've got everything you ever wanted. A handsome hippie husband, a fantastic home on wheels, and a great future ln L.A."

"Berkeley," Lorraine said sharply. "We're going to Berkeley. That's what you said."

"I know, I know, I apologize. We're going to Berkeley. I just want you to look around L.A. first. You may change your mind. L.A. is . . . groovy!" He'd been to Southern California once on a two-week vacation with his parents.

Kelly glanced at Lorraine, who shrugged her shoulders. "David is a hippie-come-lately who still uses words like *groovy*, what can I say?" Lorraine apologized for her new husband.

Lorraine reached over to straighten David's mahogany hair, which was thicker than a horse's mane and fell just as straight and long, blowing across his tanned face with the slightest breeze, though it was already a little too greasy for her tastes. A few gray hairs bristled out of the pack — David didn't tell many people he'd already done four years in the Navy before Vietnam became a dirty word. She wished valiantly this time for two haircuts — one for him, though he'd vowed never to cut his hair again.

As a lineman for Michigan Bell, he'd had to keep well-groomed. Once the two of them had decided to move to California, he began to let his hair and beard grow long and had gotten fired for it, especially when he'd pointed out to his supervisor that Alexander Graham Bell had worn a beard.

The plan had been to get fired and collect unemployment insurance by showing there was no just cause for the dismissal, but his claim had been turned down. Her cooperative apartment was supposed to have sold for at least a thousand dollars by now, but the money was never in the mail when

Lorraine's older sister forwarded it care of general delivery to the various post offices across the continent that they'd passed.

They probably didn't have six hundred left themselves to get the two of them across the border, if they hadn't had the car, Lorraine worried to herself. Their van was nearing its last legs; she hoped it would make it to Berkeley and last long enough for both of them to get jobs and more reliable wheels.

"I've got a plan," David announced. "I'll let you two guys sit in the back of the van with the curtain drawn and no lights, and we'll see if we get over the border. I warn you, if I'm asked if I have anybody else in the truck besides us, I won't lie — I don't want to spend the next couple years in jail. But if everything goes right, you're through!" All four celebrated the concept with a swig of Kool-Aid from the plastic jug Lorraine filled each day for their ice chest.

A half hour later and they'd done it! The border guard had waved them on without a search. "More Kool-Aid!" David ordered, and Lorraine slipped out of her front bucket seat and crawled over the central motor housing to enter the back where Jack and Kelly lay across the bed, Lorraine's quilt handmade by her grandmother draped loosely over them. Jack's mud-crusted boots shed gravel and dirt on the rose and blue diamond design.

"There's Rod! He made it! Stop, stop!" Jack yelled. David squealed to a halt, and the filthiest looking human being Lorraine had ever seen crawled out of the underbrush and loped toward their vehicle. Jack swung the side door open, and the creature pulled himself into the van and settled himself onto the quilt next to Kelly. The van immediately reeked.

"Thanks for stopping, man, I've been walking nonstop for days." The creature pulled out a pack of cigarettes from his dirt-encrusted backpack and lit up. Smoke almost camouflaged the other smell. Lorraine looked at David, who seemed oblivious. Especially when a new aroma drifted toward the front of the cab and a joint appeared in the space between David and Lorraine. "One toke over the line for Tok," the creature said. "Hit, anyone?" David took the smoke and inhaled deeply. Lorraine felt nauseous.

"I pass." Somebody had to stay straight enough to watch the road, Lorraine justified to herself. In reality, smoking anything made her throat choke and her eyes water.

The step van started the long incline up yet another mountain, its motor a steady hum, until the purr was interrupted with a ripping, grinding kind of squeal that ended in a heavy "thunk."

"Hey!" David yelled.

The van swerved and stopped, nearly tipping over as David pulled it off the uneven gravel and onto the soft dirt shoulder. At least there was a safe shoulder to stop on here; much of the unpaved Alkan wound through mountains that barely allowed two vehicles to pass, and the threat of road graders suddenly looming ahead in your path was always imminent.

The five travelers scrambled out, and David lay on his back and wriggled underneath the van in the dirt. After a few moments, while the others stood around in the midday August sun, he pronounced, "It's the driveshaft. Honey, get my toolbox."

Lorraine dragged the heavy metal box out from

behind David's seat and shoved it under the car. She noticed how Kelly and Jack took Rod a few hundred feet down the road to talk, their voices rising in angry spurts though she couldn't decipher any words. The way they kept looking back at her made her vaguely uneasy.

Kelly gave her a smile that was probably meant to be comforting, but it rang hollow. For some reason Lorraine pictured a mother telling a child everything was going to be all right, at the same time a burglar was beating down the door.

Even more disturbing was what this repair was going to cost, and how they were going to get it done. David was a miracle worker with that toolbox, but she was pretty sure spare driveshafts were not something you kept around like fan belts.

David emerged, covered with dirt, his black hair gritty, strong arms greasy, waving the heavy pipelike part triumphantly. "I've got a plan, honey, don't worry. I'll take the rest of the money and hitchhike to Vancouver or wherever it is that I can find a junkyard with a driveshaft that will fit, while you stay here with the food and guard the van. I don't think we should leave it alone out here in the wilderness — I've heard stories about cars getting stripped."

What about me? Lorraine whimpered inside. *Take me with you. Don't leave me alone.* Aloud she admitted, "That sounds like the only way we can do it. Are you sure the problem is the driveshaft?" He pointed out supposedly telltale marks on the metal he held; she'd have to hope he was right.

"We had too many people in the back," he whispered. "I never wanted to pick up that Rod. He's a big son of a gun, and Kelly and Jack aren't exactly tiny themselves. When he got in, on top of all that load in the back we had already, that was the last straw. It's a wonder we still have springs and shocks."

"Are those parts okay?" Lorraine asked in alarm. He'd already replaced their starter in Winnipeg and their manifold in Calgary.

"So far. But we're going to have to get rid of this crowd. Maybe it's a good thing this happened. Pack me a big lunch, okay, honey?"

Obediently she dug in the cooler and made bologna sandwiches with the last of the lunch meat and bread and put them in a brown paper bag. She could live for weeks on the canned stews, hashes, and baked beans in the hand-built cupboard. As he added their last cans of juices to the bag and pocketed their stash of dollars, a Jeep stopped.

"Car trouble?" The driver leaned over and swung open the passenger door. David got in, a wide smile on his face for his rescuer and for Lorraine.

"Wow, that was good timing! Take care of the truck now," David said as the Jeep drove away.

Not even an "I love you, take care of yourself." No time. He would have if there had been more time.

Kelly jogged back to the van, her braid flopping behind her. Lorraine was in shock at how fast everything had happened.

"Yeah, rides are easy to get out here in the wild when you're standing by a disabled vehicle," Kelly said. She turned and glared pointedly in the direction of Rod and Jack. "The boys are going to go on ahead themselves from here, aren't you?"

Her voice was insistent, demanding. Rod kept looking at the toes of his scuffed combat boots. Jack's glance kept shifting between Rod and Kelly, his face unreadable to Lorraine.

To Lorraine's amazement, the next car to appear also stopped. "Get in, you two," Kelly ordered, and the men climbed into the sedan's rear seat, behind a shaggy gray-haired couple in flannel shirts who clucked in sympathy at their plight.

The woman kept motioning for Kelly and Lorraine to climb in, too — "There's always plenty of room for people with car trouble," she said. "We have to take care of each other out here in the wilderness." Her bearded mate nodded.

It looked to Lorraine as if Jack was keeping a strong grip on Rod's upper arm.

The driver finally believed the women really intended to stay there and drove off. Kelly breathed a huge sigh of relief, flinging her head and arms up to the sky, then turned to Lorraine with carefully phrased words:

"Rod had a gun. He was going to rip you off of everything he could carry."

Lorraine stared. Suddenly she felt very alone, even with Kelly's presence. Kelly slipped an arm around her to hold Lorraine steady.

"There, there, it's going to be all right now."

Yeah, with the burglar kicking in the door downstairs, Lorraine envisioned. She leaned into Kelly's leather-vested chest. At least Kelly washed regularly, too. She even smelled sweet, kind of like nutmeg. Lorraine could feel the soft give of Kelly's rounded breasts against hers. She felt woozy, while another memory wafted in and out of her mind like a shadow.

"What are the chances they're coming back?" Lorraine had to ask, her face buried in Kelly's gauzy yellow shirt and leather vest.

"Zero," Kelly said promptly. "I told them I'd cut their balls off if either of them tried." She brandished a Swiss army knife. "Hey, I'd do it, too, don't think I wouldn't, if I had to," she said in response to Lorraine's gasp.

"Isn't Jack your boyfriend?"

"Well, yeah, we sort of traveled together the past few months, but we were going to split up in Seattle anyway. He's got friends in Montana, and I'm heading to my sister's in Sausalito. I've just about had enough of the road. I lied about her not sending me more money — cashier's check is on its way to Whitehorse. She's been keeping track of my bank account forever. There's still some left, but it's getting low enough that I have to think about going to work."

Lorraine explained about the thousand dollars still tied up in the sale of her co-op, and about how she couldn't go to her parents for any money since they had four younger children still at home. She'd never thought about not working again, if she ever got to magical Berkeley, which had seemed to be the center of all the wonderful changes happening on television every night. "How long have you been traveling and not working?"

"Six years. Don't look so astonished. Since

nineteen sixty-four, when I got out of college. When
Dad died he left us both a little bit of money. She
bought a house; I hit the road. I've got better
memories; she's still got a house. I wouldn't trade."

"So what will you do in Sausalito?"

"Maybe I can find a job and set up an apartment
for a change. Anywhere in the Bay area, maybe even
Berkeley, though its time has passed."

"What do you mean?"

"Don't get shook — you think Berkeley is hippie
heaven, right? Those days are dying fast. Last time I
went by Haight-Ashbury, kids were OD'ing like flies,
and there was more crime than New York City.
Everybody's too stoned to care anymore, or else
they're out for their own buck, their own power. This
is nineteen-seventy, a new decade."

Lorraine almost felt like crying. Kelly's arms
tightened around her.

"Hey, what's the matter, little one? You think you
missed it? The sixties happened and you weren't
ready? Don't worry, you didn't miss a thing. I don't
think you were cut out to be a hippie anyway.
Neither is that dumb fuck husband of yours."

The words hit Lorraine with a jolt; rather than
anger, she felt immense relief. The emperor had no
clothes. She laughed aloud and kept on laughing,
burying her face in Kelly's shoulder and the nutmeg
aroma that reminded her of her mother's bread
pudding.

"There, there. I hope you don't mind that I called
him a dumb fuck, but he is, posturing around with
all that hair like a lion. Ordering you around like a
maid. Leaving you alone to protect his precious van.
Don't worry, *I'm* not going to leave you."

Lorraine was flooded by waves of feelings — relief, gratitude, fear of what would happen next, comfort in Kelly's arms. And something else she pushed aside. She drew herself upright and wiped away her tears. Okay, life went on. So what came next? She was aware of heat where Kelly's arm still rested around her shoulders. She didn't pull away until the heat became unbearable.

She stood up straight and walked back toward the van, Kelly following. "What kind of job are you going to look for?" she finally asked Kelly as she opened the side door and straightened things up inside. Kelly helped her shake out the quilt.

"Anything for starters," Kelly said. "A bookstore, coffee house. The dream job would be on a small newspaper — I majored in English. I sure would like a good bed every night. This sleeping bag is for the birds." She unrolled her backpack. "Whew, it stinks."

Lorraine giggled. "That's what I hate most about the road — keeping clean."

"I told you, you're no hippie. And neither is that phony baloney hubby of yours."

Lorraine had a brief urge to defend him somehow, but it passed. Take care of the truck, indeed. He really was a phony baloney. She giggled at the phrase. If they'd been real hippies, they'd have lived the life in Detroit on Plum Street, instead of thinking they had to go to California to be free. Why had she felt something was missing from her life — "the meaning of life," in David's words — that going on the road with David would fix? It hadn't. The marriage was over before it got started, a mistake that she should have foreseen. And what in the world did that mean for her future?

She shivered. "So are you going to go on now, too?"

"Nope, I told you, I'm staying here with you. If that fool husband of yours thinks you can be left here all alone, he's dumber than I thought. You don't know the first thing about living out in the wilderness. What did you do before this trip, anyway?"

"I was a nurse. So don't you tell me I don't know how to live by my wits. I know a few things too."

"Yeah, sure, if you need to start an IV. Can you tell a cranberry from a poisonous berry? Do you know how to keep bears away?"

Oh my God, the lean, mean grizzly she'd seen leaping across the Alkan in a single bound, nothing like the fat cuddly-looking black bears back in Michigan. Kelly reached out for her again, and this time Lorraine let herself melt into the woman's body. She'd never survive this.

"You're trembling." It was a statement, not an accusation the way David would have made it. She didn't even try to stop. Tears began to pour down her face and into Kelly's gauzy shirt under the vest. "There, there," Kelly told her over and over, stroking her back, kneading her shoulders, smoothing her hair.

Lorraine kept feeling something else that made her forget about bears and abandonment. The tightening in the groin, the awareness of her breasts. There was no other word for it, she was feeling sexually aroused! What the hell was that all about? A wave of panic hit her. Then she realized that it was only normal, a human body reacts to nice touching no matter who's doing it, don't worry.

She pulled away from Kelly anyway and tugged

her sweatshirt down over her jeans and straightened her hair. Once again she wished she'd had a good haircut but brushed away that thought as irrelevant and stupid.

The important fact is that I'm alone in Alaska with only a woman and a knife to protect me, a target for anybody who drives by and wants to strip the van, waiting who knows how long for David while he chases all over the Yukon Territory and British Columbia looking for a driveshaft that may or may not be the only problem the van has anyway. And the marriage is a mistake. David is a dolt.

The tears started again. This time she let Kelly envelop her and rock her gently. "There, there," Kelly whispered. Even if that burglar was kicking in the door, the little girl inside Lorraine felt her mother would somehow protect her. And make her bread pudding.

When the tears stopped, Kelly said, "Are you all right now?" Lorraine nodded, feeling a little sheepish. Kelly touched her once on the cheek and said, "Okay, let's get organized." They made an inventory of the food and the gaps in the menu for two weeks, the minimum time Kelly thought David might be gone. Not enough cans to last, not even for one, though there was a giant bag of pancake mix that could feed them a month. There was plenty of propane for the camp stove, and Kelly knew how to build fires to roast the food she said she'd catch.

"There's a river running along the road near here and it's full of salmon," Kelly pointed over her shoulder. "I saw you have fishing poles in the van."

Automatically, Lorraine shook her head no. "We don't have a license for here."

"Hey, what judge is going to convict a woman abandoned on her honeymoon with only salmon to live on just because she didn't have a license? But you keep an eye out for rangers, okay?" Kelly pretended to put binoculars to her eyes and scan the landscape. They were surrounded by hundreds of miles of dense forest and snowcapped mountains, without a trace of civilization two yards away from the road. Lorraine had to laugh.

That night they had salmon, hush puppies from the pancake mix, and a salad of sorts of wild greens, put together by Kelly, who'd grilled the fish over an open fire. Lorraine had never tasted anything so good. They heated water over the fire and gave themselves sponge baths and washed out clothes and laid them over bushes to dry. Kelly put her cap back on and switched to a loose flannel shirt so that she would look like a man to passersby.

"I'd recommend you do the same, but there's no way you can hide those curves," she said, making Lorraine feel embarrassed but glad. Sometimes David had made snide remarks about her being too fat.

Kelly laid her aired-out sleeping bag on the ground next to the van.

"You can't sleep out there — it gets too cold at night!" Lorraine said.

"No room on the floor inside," Kelly shrugged.

"Don't be ridiculous — sleep with me." Even as she said the words, Lorraine felt her stomach tighten. No, nothing would happen. This woman wasn't after her body. How would a woman do something like that anyway? The fears ran through her mind, and she dismissed them one by one. She meant it purely innocently. Of course Kelly would take it that way.

And Kelly did, night after night, sleeping well on her side of the six-foot-square bed, after exhausting days filled with discovering a different Alaska than David had shown her from the road. By day, Lorraine was in Kelly's arms more than once, leaning for support as they climbed up mountain crags and over rocky brooks, huddling for warmth when they both fell in the icy water.

Lorraine was having the best time of her life, finally enjoying herself on her honeymoon, even if the bridegroom was absent. She liked the way Kelly looked at her, the way Kelly was really with her, the way Kelly's hands felt on her skin. She sneaked peeks at Kelly when she thought Kelly wasn't looking, wondering at the same time why she felt she had to hide her stares. And sometimes she caught Kelly looking at her in exactly the same way, and it made her tingle inside. There was no doubt about it, this was sexual. The thought scared her less and less as she got used to it.

In her mind she let herself consider the frightening possibilities. She couldn't be gay, she was married. She'd dated plenty of men and slept with two of them, though neither of them had been what she'd hoped. Her mother had assured her that sex would be almost mystical, magical, a final melding of two into one. So far it had never happened.

In her heart of hearts Lorraine had to admit that she'd married David because she was feeling old at twenty-seven, and she hadn't been able to get up the courage to move to the San Francisco area across the entire continent on her own. David had said from the day she'd met him that he was moving to California, and he might have been her last chance.

Only maybe there might be other chances.

On one chilly night she let herself snuggle close to Kelly in bed. "I'm really glad I'm not sleeping outside on the ground tonight," Kelly said. "Hey, your hands are like ice! Here, tuck them in here." And she took Lorraine's two hands and put them under her own breasts. Lorraine yanked them away and sat bolt upright in bed.

"Sorry, I didn't mean anything. It's just that I always put my cold hands under my boobs when I'm freezing. Look, I didn't mean anything. I'll sleep outside if you want. I'm sorry, really." Kelly got out of bed and began to get dressed.

Lorraine watched her. With all her heart she wanted Kelly back in her bed. And with more than her heart.

"Can . . . can I ask you one question?"

"Sure." Kelly stopped, one bare leg arched over her jeans. Lorraine couldn't help staring at the perfect curve of Kelly's calf, at the smooth line of her thigh.

"Have . . . have you ever slept with a woman?"

"Sure, we've been sleeping together for a week."

"That's not what I mean!" Lorraine's face was flushed.

"I know, I had to tease you." Kelly dared to reach out one finger to touch Lorraine's hot cheek. "Yes, I'm gay. Jack was mostly a traveling companion, though we had sex a couple of times when we were both stoned. During college and on the road I've made love to a lot of people, men and women, and I prefer women."

"A lot of women?" Lorraine had to ask it.

"Hey, I told you, I'm ready to settle down. I've

been thinking about it for a while, aiming myself toward my sister's to use her place as a home base till I get settled. And then you came along, and you wanted to go to the same part of the country, and I started to wonder if maybe it wasn't a sign. That maybe we should be going to San Francisco together."

"Maybe we should." Lorraine smiled. And then she remembered. The girl who had transferred to Lorraine's junior high just as her friends were starting to hold mixed parties, just as the girls were starting to practice kissing one another to rehearse for the real thing, kissing boys. Only when Lorraine had kissed B.J. Barnes, it hadn't been a rehearsal.

B.J., who'd worn her hair in a DA like Elvis Presley and who was the first to adopt torn tight jeans and her father's shirts as her after-school uniform and who taught Lorraine the chicken, which got them sent off the school dance floor for dirty dancing.

B.J., who'd slow-danced with Lorraine in her parents' rec room basement to "Earth Angel" by the Penguins and whose hands inside Lorraine's angora sweater had made Lorraine melt, like a boy's roaming hands had never done.

B.J., whose parents had sent her away to Casa Maria Home for Wayward Girls.

Lorraine had gotten a clear message from B.J.'s imprisonment. A message that had sent her back to boys.

She told Kelly the story, while Kelly kissed her hair and stroked her forehead and twisted strands of her hair into tendrils that tickled her ear.

"It's a new day, I keep telling you," Kelly said. "The seventies are going to be different. There's going to be a place for you and me. And I think that someplace around Berkeley is exactly where we'll find it."

Kelly's hands roamed Lorraine's shoulders and back, staying on safe ground while both of them knew where those hands wanted to be. Finally Lorraine lay back on the bed, conscious of how the cotton fibers of the T-shirt she slept in were rasping like files against her nipples. She had to look down over her chin at her chest: Rock-hard peaks jutted upward through the shirt. Kelly followed her glance and laughed aloud. "Let me make love to you, Lorraine," she said in a low whisper.

Lorraine felt her body stiffen, but it was like trying to immobilize a wave midflow. A tidal wave. She reached up and grabbed Kelly to her and pulled the woman onto her. Kelly was squirming, shedding her pants and shirt. Lorraine rolled aside, slipped off her own clothes, and drew Kelly to her once more. The aroma of nutmeg flowed over her warm skin. *This is how it should feel. This is what I've always wanted.*

They lay together for what felt like a millennium, bringing about a new life between them as surely as if a baby were being conceived. This new being, this paired oneness that left both of them whole while creating a separate new life, was the two of them in one, both in each other. Their own holy trinity. They were forming a mystery between them that would take a lifetime to understand. It would be fully worth the time.

As Kelly explored the crevices and creases of her body, Lorraine quivered and floated in pleasure, the feelings like red-hot lava. Their intensity was burying her, smothering her for one molten moment. She was sure she would erupt in flames before she burst through the heat and into her own flowing consciousness.

She was eternal essence of woman, rippling through the ages like an all-knowing goddess claiming her own in the endless moment of creating. An ever-widening universe.

Her body took in all pleasure, all feeling, all sensation, and sent it back to the world as pure joy. She lay there bathed in eternal good, the fullness of consciousness, complete and completed, awash in white-light sensations that didn't ebb away so much as sink in, penetrate, until she was fully, totally satiated.

And still Kelly's tongue swirled on her clitoris as if she were enjoying her first and last supper in one ever-lasting feast.

They would find a way. David would come back, and she would insist he drive both of them to Sausalito while he could go on to L.A. and live his phony-baloney life as a hippie-come-lately. Or they could leave now and let him come back to his precious van in whatever shape vandals might leave it. Her co-op would sell, and her thousand dollars would catch up to her eventually. There was nothing among her possessions under the bed that was of any value to her at all, not now. Or she could travel on with Kelly forever, if they found that was real freedom. Whichever. She and Kelly together, forever. They would find a way.

She gently eased Kelly over and began her own tentative, first exploration into the meaning of life.

A Seven-Turtle Day

Catherine Ennis

Rain from farther north had swollen the tiny river that ran under the highway to town. The runoff had caused a small roadside pond to deepen and form a shallow lake on the right side of the road. I slowed the car after crossing the highway culvert, looking across the pond for the fallen cypress log that jutted from the muddy bank. "There," I said aloud. "One big, two medium, one small." My smile broadened; I resumed the moderate speed at which I drove to work.

"Work" was the myriad of bookkeeping events necessary to show the area's largest feed and seed store in the recognizable black. Five days a week, for sixteen years, I've climbed dusty stairs to gain entrance to a loft that overlooks the store's selling floor and houses three desks, a large safe for fire protection of the precious records, and a tiny partitioned area without a door, which is called my office.

For eleven of those years, I've been manager of the three-person accounting force, taking solely upon myself the job of paymaster, a weekly event necessitating a walk of two blocks down Main Street to the local bank. In the past, that chore has simply meant a welcome Friday break. Now, unaccountably, I felt a breath of excitement thinking about that trip to the bank. The feeling was akin to what I had felt as a child when anticipating mighty events like the circus or an afternoon at the double-feature movie.

Usually, I'd leave the office at noon, bank bag and purse under my arm, and eat a leisurely meal at Lily's cafe, sometimes taking fifteen minutes over our allotted lunchtime. After lunch I'd stroll to the bank, transact my business, then saunter back to the store. I did not consider the extra few minutes as stolen from my employer since I was the person who locked the doors in the evening, usually waiting ten or fifteen minutes past the closing hour for browsers to leave. If today's plan did not go awry, I might be adding half an hour or more to my lunch time.

I spent considerable time dressing this morning. For some years we've been allowed to wear slacks to work, but on this day I chose a dark, straight skirt that makes me look thinner than I am, pumps that give me an inch of height over the flat shoes I usually wear, and a frilly blouse with long sleeves.

When I walked past the loading dock on my way to the store's rear door, I expected and received approving whistles from the men lounging there. This did not disturb me in the least. There wasn't one of them under fifty, and I'd seen them every day for years. My smile wasn't for them, however. Today I planned to take a bold step in changing my life. Perhaps it wasn't a giant step but, shy as I am, it was out of character for me to take any step at all. *I know she'll say yes,* I thought. After all, there were four turtles on the log this morning.

Both Mother and Aunt Orey had commented on my looks. "Think you're a movie star, girlie?" and, "Whatcha gettin' all dressed up for? Got a date?" Well, I'm too plain to be in the movies, and I gave up on dating a long time ago. So what could I answer when I wasn't exactly sure, myself, what it was I had in mind?

Eleanor Biddle was already at her desk, already drinking a Coke and dumping salted peanuts in her mouth before each swallow. That was her breakfast. As I passed, she gave me a friendly wave, her slurping and crunching noises following me into my tiny office.

It was a few minutes before eight, four hours to go before lunch. Unaccountably, my heart was thumping with excitement. I needed to take many deep breaths in order to slow it. This Friday wasn't to be any different from Fridays past, I told myself. I liked Dot very much, and if I wanted her for a friend, I had to let her know. Today I was going to let her know.

I had planned to wait until nine to make my call, but my hand reached for the phone when it was straight-up eight o'clock. "Pharmacy," I heard, "May I help you?"

"I, ah, have a prescription to be filled."

"Do you have a number?"

"Yes." I gave the number and name, then I said, "Dot, it's me, Maude." And before I could say the casual sort of unconcerned things I'd planned to say, to kind of lead into it, I blurted, "Will you eat lunch with me today?"

"Sure, I'd like that. What time do you eat?"

I almost forgot to ask what time. It had been so easy, and she hadn't hesitated at all. "Sure," she'd said, "Sure."

"I thought we'd go to the Bayou Cafe and sit outside on the deck. Does that sound okay?" I looked through the door, but Eleanor wasn't paying any attention. She was brushing peanut crumbs off her desk, washing her mouth with the last swallow of Coke.

"I can only take an hour. Maybe we should call first and place our order; they're pretty slow."

"Good idea." I said, "If you like seafood, we can both order the Friday special."

We settled on noon, the lunch special, and that I would pick her up.

Now that I had asked her, I wondered why I'd waited so long. She had been transferred from New Orleans to our small town two months ago, and I'd seen her at least once a week since then. Mama or Aunt Orey always had a prescription that needed filling, and it was my job to see that neither of them ran out of whatever it was.

I hadn't paid much attention to the new pharmacist, but I began to notice that she was paying attention to me. Her smile seemed extra friendly, and she always had a few words about something other than the prescription. It wasn't long until she knew where I worked, that my mother and aunt lived with me, and that I'd never been married. She wasn't wearing a ring, so I assumed she wasn't either.

I did have a few friends, all married, and all with many small children to accompany us wherever we went. This was not to my liking, so today I deliberately set out to make a friend of the new person in town. Also, there was something about her — I can't say what — that attracted me. I liked to see her smile, hear her laugh, watch her bang the register with her fist to open the cash drawer. There wasn't anything about her I didn't like, so I looked forward to our lunch together.

She ate with an appetite that matched mine, and I would have stayed there all day except for the payroll. I did tell her about the turtles. "The more turtles on the log, the better the day," I said. "There were four this morning."

"So this is a good day?" Her laughter was genuine. She reached across the table and put her warm hand on mine. "It's been a good day for me, Maude." she said. "I'm glad you called."

Flustered, my heart racing again, I didn't know what to say. We rode in silence back to town. When I stopped the car she leaned over, her face close to mine, and said, "I enjoyed our lunch. Let's do it again."

"I can't take over an hour for lunch every day," I

answered, "but we can certainly meet at Lily's. They're near and fast, and the food's pretty good."

"The company's good, too." With a quick nod, she got out of the car and crossed the sidewalk to the drugstore. I watched until the doors closed behind her, my mouth as dry as dust.

There were no complaints about the payroll, so I guess I didn't goof up. Back home, Aunt Orey complained because I forgot to bring her medicine with me. "Dressing pretty must do something bad to your memory, girl."

"I'll just have to go back to the store tomorrow." I was thinking that Dot sometimes works half a day on Saturday. Maybe she'd go to lunch again. We wouldn't have to eat in a hurry this time.

When Dot saw me at the prescription counter, she actually beamed. "Hi, there," she smiled, "I've been thinking about you."

"You have?" I asked.

"Yep. Wouldn't this be a great day to drive over to Winston for lunch? I get off at noon, so if you're free we could eat at that country buffet I'm always hearing about."

I was free, of course, so that's what we did. Not only that Saturday but, after a few weeks, we were meeting regularly at Lily's each noon. Dot usually remembered to ask about the turtles. "So I'll know what kind of day I'm having," she'd explain.

I began to feel that I'd known her all my life. Some evenings we'd get takeouts and eat in her motel room. She was the traveling pharmacist for a drug chain, staying in a store as long as needed, then moving within the state to another town, another store. This caused me some concern at first, but I

didn't want to think about her leaving so I didn't
dwell on it.

Mother and Aunt Orey were miffed because I was
away so much. Aunt Orey would ask, "What do you
and that woman do?"

"We eat, we talk, we go to the show in Winston."
What could I say? Should I tell them the feeling I
had when we shared an armrest and our shoulders
touched, or when Dot's hand closed over mine at the
scary part? I would hold as still as a board so as not
to break the contact. Dot didn't seem to notice, but
she touched a lot.

One Friday evening when we were settled on her
bed, propped up by pillows and a chair cushion,
eating pizza and watching the weekly fright movie,
she leaned across me to reach for pizza on the
bedside table. I almost choked when I felt her weight
resting on my thighs. The pizza slices were gummed
together by cheese so it wasn't easy to separate
them. She tugged for a moment, then gave up and
collapsed in my lap.

Laughing, and turning so that she was lying on
her back, she said softly, "We have to quit meeting
like this, Maudie dear; what would people say?"

Oh yes, I knew what she meant. She was teasing,
but I knew what her words meant. Anyone peeping
through the window would see two women in a
darkened room, lying together on a tousled bed,
probably doing lesbian things to each other. I wanted
to say something clever, but nothing clever came to
mind. We stared at each other, and the silence grew.

"Maudie," Dot finally whispered, "dear Maudie."

Her words were like a caress, "Maudie, dear
Maudie." I had never been addressed as anything

other than just plain Maude. I looked down at her, felt my heart beat faster and my entire body flood with an emotion I had not experienced before.

"Do you care for me?" she asked quietly, her eyes deep and liquid.

"Care for you?" I was almost stuttering. "Care for you?" I asked again.

Dot slid from my lap, pushed herself into a sitting position, and leaned so that our faces were almost touching. "Yes," she said, "I want to know if you care for me, because I certainly care for you."

What to say? It took a few moments for my head to clear enough that I could make my mouth move. Dot waited, one eyebrow raised slightly, her lips not quite closed. "Yes," I managed. "Yes, I care for you. I care a lot."

"Ummm." Just that one hushed sound, but it held meanings that I understood. Dot leaned closer. I could feel her warmth. "Okay," she said, "I know how to handle that."

I have no firsthand experience but I do read, and I had an instant flash of Dot's warm breasts cupped in my hands. I lowered my gaze. And then, unbidden, I had another flash of us naked on the bed. It was very hard for me to clear my mind of the image the two of us made, tangled together in the dark.

With a movement as smooth and natural as if we'd practiced it for years, our lips met. It was a tiny kiss, like that of friends, but it left my heart thumping. She pulled away slowly, her breath sweet on my face.

"I'd like more, Maudie." Her words caused my face to flame. I opened my mouth to say that I wanted more, too, but before I could speak she was whispering softly in my ear.

"Slide down, Maudie. Lie on your back so we can make love."

Now, incapable of speech of any kind, I simply did as she asked. I pushed myself from the headboard and slid toward the foot of the bed.

Our next kiss was long. She breathed into me, tasting my mouth. Her tongue was soft and wet and warm, and I stopped being afraid.

My earlier vision caused my hands to reach for her breasts and she gave them to me. I lay with my eyes closed, Dot leaning over me, and my hands were alive with the feel of her soft flesh. Soon Dot moved away, undid the fastenings of her blouse, then moved so that her naked breasts were available to my mouth. As if I had done it a thousand times, I took a nipple between my lips and began sucking.

My mouth claiming one breast, my hand caressing the other, I was soon lost in an explosion of sensations; those smooth, warm mounds — so available, so delicious.

I almost cried out when she pulled away. "We have to undress, Maudie." She began fumbling with the buttons on my blouse, her breathing heavy.

I have never wanted anything more than I wanted to feel her nakedness, and for her to feel mine. My clothes came off in seconds, were thrown to the floor, and I lay uncovered and unclothed, my arms reaching for whatever part of her was available.

"Whoa, darling, we have plenty of time." Her words didn't calm me. I wanted, I *needed,* her touch between my legs. I took her wrist and guided her hand down my body. When I felt her fingers move through wetness, I pulled her hand tight against me, my hips jerking out of all control.

I felt her fingers sliding through moisture; then I felt her enter me. I had been waiting all of my life to utter the "Ahaaa . . ." that came from deep within, a sound of my complete satisfaction.

Climax was a word I had read, a something wonderful that happened to other people when engaging in sex. It was an experience I had never shared, so I had no idea what it was like. My climax, the first, was like nothing else on earth.

Dot's fingers would dip into me; then, after a moment, withdraw to stroke through heat and wetness, to circle my clitoris gently. Then she would slide back down into me, pushing harder, deeper, her fingers in motion.

Oh, how I enjoyed the feel of her! "Don't stop!" I pleaded. "Please don't stop!"

I heard her breath coming in gasps, felt her body moving in rhythm with mine. Then, for an instant, I felt a gathering, a swelling, as if everything in me was bunching together, as if her hand and my flesh had been welded, had become one and the same. Her hand, her moving fingers, felt huge inside me. My hips stilled, their movement no longer necessary. Dot had filled me to overflowing and I came in a gush — a gush of moisture, of release, a feeling so intense that I cried out in both pain and pure physical delight.

Dot held me, her hand still between my legs, her other arm supporting my head. She leaned to kiss, her tongue in my mouth, then in my ear, her teeth raking my nipple.

"Goodness, Maudie, but you're a wild one!"

My breathing almost normal, I said, "Dot, I've wanted to be loved for so long. I didn't know it'd be like this."

"I know," she said. "I could tell."

"You're the only person who's ever — ever touched me. I think I must have been the stupidest virgin on earth."

Dot withdrew her hand, letting her fingers play in my pubic hair, causing me to tense. "No, Maudie, not stupid, just inexperienced." She paused. "Not inexperienced any more are you?"

"Will you let me touch you?"

Dot sighed. "I thought you'd never ask," she said.

By the time we finally had enough lovemaking, I didn't think I'd be able to walk to the bathroom. Dot propped herself on pillows to watch me dress, her eyes dreamy, her expression smug.

"Tomorrow's Saturday, and I'm not working in the morning. Why don't I pick you up around nine? We'll drive to the coast, do a little gambling, spend the night and come home Sunday."

The gambling part didn't thrill me, but spending the whole night in a motel miles away from home was too good to miss. "I'll be ready at nine," I said, grinning from ear to ear.

Our good-bye was long, involving much kissing and touching. Once home in bed, I began to relive the evening. I don't think I slept at all.

Dot was prompt. She made instant friends with Mom and Aunt Orey, telling them about their medications, asking about their health, showing a genuine interest. They were charmed, both waving cheerful good-byes from the porch as we drove away.

I kind of hugged my side of the seat, not so sure

as the night before. I was in love with her, and that
made everything she said to me sound like an
invitation to jump into bed. Maybe she only wanted
to gamble today and tonight. Maybe it wasn't seemly
to talk about what we'd done. Maybe we weren't
going to love each other again, even though all I
wanted was for her to suck my breasts, enter me
with her busy fingers, do things to me with her
tongue.

It wasn't until we were out of sight of the house,
and I felt her hand claim mine, that last night began
to seem real.

We crossed the highway culvert and I looked at
the pond, counting. "Dot," I exclaimed, "seven! There,
see them! Seven on the log!"

"Oh, Lordy, that's the most ever isn't it?" She
patted my thigh. "Does that mean what I think it
means?"

I covered her hand with both of mine to show
that I welcomed her touch. "It means today is going
to be one we'll remember. We'll probably win
millions!" I squeezed to show my excitement, at the
same time pressing her hand firmly to my thigh.

"Winning can wait, Maudie, but I suddenly find
that I can't. I'm driving straight to the motel as fast
as I can." She turned her head to look at me,
eyebrows questioning. Did her words meet with my
approval?

Not hesitating, I said, "That's what I hoped you'd
do." Gulping, because my throat had gone very dry, I
added, "You know what a seven-turtle day means,
don't you?"

Her attention now on the road, she nodded. "Oh,
yes, Maudie dear. Oh, yes."

Time Exposure

Teresa Stores

genesis

I am thirty.

Void. Fog swirls in the night, a spirit — God —
dipping down to touch the backs of my folded hands,
my face. I am alone in this universe, lying on a
wooden dock. I am thirty, newly divorced, empty. The
waters of the lake move, lap gently at the pilings in
the swampy darkness below.

I am thinking of women.

I open the shutter and sit again at my desk. Light and shadow separate, become image on my paper, folding over, layering. I am trying to document time. One time. I am trying to place a first time in time.

But time repeats itself, resonates in on itself. I am thirty; I am twenty-five; I am nineteen; twelve; ten; eight. Each time, a first time.

I am twenty-five.

She and I stand, gasping, light-headed, in the sky in this first time. Our first 14,000-foot mountain.

We passed up through clouds to get here, cold fog swirling around our ankles, the backs of our necks. I climbed watching her calf, the curve of her thigh, the pale shadow where skin disappears beneath the fabric of her shorts, just ahead of me, just out of reach across that gray mist, higher and higher.

I smell her sweat, and something else, where oxygen is not.

Now she smiles, holding her arms out against the vault of sky, mountains receding into watery blue, her smile and curve, her breasts and hips divided from me only by this thin air, sweet with her scent, and I gasp again, trying to breathe, this first time of seeing heaven.

* * * * *

I am ten.

She and I explore deep into the swamp behind
our suburban tract houses, imagining ourselves in a
primeval forest, beings before beings, poised between
earth and water, back at the beginning of time. Our
sneakers are black with mud, soggy where we sink
into the muck. We sweat in the silence of Florida
midday, limp with damp, almost a part of the air.

I circle a cypress tree, balancing on its knobby
knees, hugging soft bark, sweet smell, the feminine
curves of the trunk, precarious between brown water
and dry land.

She follows, her fingertips brushing mine. I hear a
trill, feel it in my arm, my chest, though the cicadas
are still silent. My fingers tingle as if some lush
green things, vines like snakes, grow from them.

I am nineteen.

She and I lie in the dark on our mattress-on-the-
floor beds and watch the moon rise, the sun rise,
through our curtainless window in this first time. We
are roommates, the first time either of us has lived
away from home.

I dream of bodies in a bruised sky. Starry
peepholes. I watch her rise through the shades of my
lashes, glide around the room, her skin the soft
white-gold of the moon, crescent curves of calf, thigh,
buttocks, belly, breasts, hips. She cannot look directly
at me, but she knows I am here; I see it in her
circling. I feel the pull, like sand sucking at my feet.

The sun streams suddenly into the room, and I

am full awake. Squinting. Hot in the wrong season. I have slept through the signs separating night from day.

I am eight.

She and I flap the wings of our white robes. We are first birds, flying up and down the church hallway, swooping like pelicans over the breakers, snatching fish from the surf, until the deacon gives us a stern look, shushes us. We can hear the organ trill in the sanctuary, lapping water in the baptismal pool, someone praying. He schools us, a flock of two, to the top of the stairs. Our first time baptized.

The pastor stands like a piling in the blue water. The congregation is blurry and streaked through the glass. She looks at me, her eyes wide, glassy. I see, now we will be fish. I think, now we will be saved.

The deacon takes her hand and gives it to the pastor, helping her down the steps. Her wings flow out wide in the clear pool, and she looks back at me, lost, no longer sure we can fly.

I hear the pastor's voice like a submarine's sonar bouncing from the bottom up. I watch him dunk my friend under, baptizing her, and I see her swim, an undersea bird, a fish with wings. Her hair spreads out like jellyfish.

And suddenly the deacon hooks my hand and passes it to the pastor. My robe billows out like gills filtering air. My feet no longer touch bottom. And I am pushed under, sucking in water, burning with chlorine, a sea monster.

I see, clear through the blur of water, her,

looking down at me, her small nipples hard against the wet of her robe. I think, now, saved.

I am twelve.

She and I ride bareback, my arms around her thin waist, my small breasts bumping against her spine, our hips rocking together. We are part of the horse, part animal.

We play house in her hayloft, even though we are almost too old, smelling of horse and sweat and swamp, dust motes glittering in the cracks of light between boards. I come home from work, the husband, and she, the wife, kisses me hello.

We spend the night in my single bed, wrestling, tickling, rocking as if we are part of the horse, riding bareback.

In the morning, we smell of animals.

I am thirty.

The fog is clearing, thinning to light. I watch the cypress trees curve in and out of shadows, listen to the lake laughing. A white-gold moon disrobes, veils dissipating in the first rays of sun. A white heron skims the surface, mirrored, and I feel the dock shake: a gator or catfish bumping the pilings below. Horses begin to neigh on the other side, and the air is damp and thickening with the morning smells of beasts and hay.

I am thinking of women. Creation. I am rested, and it is good.

new testament

I find myself staring at the page, the words. Light floods my desk, and the women, the images, the words are stark and black in that white, paper glare.

I've become lost in the writing — the women — again, lost in those intervals that skip, like a scratched record, across space and time. It has been this way since the beginning, since the first words, since the first time. In all those first times.

In the morning, we smell of animals. *I am twelve.* She draws a heart under my bed. She writes in permanent marker. I love you.

We balance on the knobs of cypress knees. My fingertips tingle, as if there are words singing in the nerves like cicadas, and I want to reach around the sweet soft tree to touch her again. But, *I am ten.* Instead I say, Let's just go a little farther, and I leap for an island across the water.

She looks at me and screams, still balanced on the cypress knees, the other side of the creek. Snake! Snake!

I look away from her, my sneakers wet and cold, sinking into muck, my chest tightening. Behind me on my island in the swamp, there are only twisted black vines. No snake.

But she runs anyway, screaming through the swamp, and I stand still, alone, held by the tingling

in my hand, feet sucked into cool wet sand, and then
I scream too.

The preacher says, Now you are saved, baptized. *I
am eight.*
My friend echoes, Saved.
As they bow their heads and begin to pray, I
stare at the white outline of her panties through her
wet robe, her tiny nipples hard against the cloth. I
want to pray with them, but my tongue is thick. The
words are liquid and if I open my mouth, I know I
will drown.

I am in a lake of women, leaning against a post
as if moored, mute, the beer bottle in my hand
sweaty, warm. I don't want to be fuzzy with drink; I
am already drunk with women dancing, women
talking, women. It's my first time in a lesbian bar. *I
am thirty.*
She stands beside me. Smiles. Speaks. Hi.
I find my voice. Hi.
Our words are stark, soft, light, and dark.
I am thirty, divorced. alone. I am a writer.

My roommate and I trill a lyric into the first
light of day, lying in our separate mattress-on-the-
floor beds. We taste new words, new ideas, new
language: men, women, God, sex, dreams, words. I

am a writer. I am a poet. I am an artist. Home. High school. College. Today. Yesterday. The foreign places we will go tomorrow, loading our cars or our backpacks and just going. Dreams.

I want to say, I have dreamed of you, I felt your pull as if a tide in a swamp. *I am nineteen.* I write a poem instead.

Our tongues are dancing a language for which I have no words. The bar is rushing away; time rushes in on itself. *I am twelve; I am thirty; I am without end.*

It is the first kiss.

Oh, god. I am here and not here. She is me. I am writing her a sonnet in this kiss.

She stops. Smiles. I am gasping, lost in her tongue her mouth her lips... Time. She looks into the rearview mirror, dabs at the edges of her mouth. We should go back into the bar.

I close my eyes for a second, a minute, a year, in the lullaby of her voice. As we wind words around each other, around the men in our lives 14,000 feet below. We are each married. *I am twenty-five.*

Have you ever thought about sex with women?

No, my words all say no, too loud, too soft, tracing the curve of her breast, climbing the inside of her thigh, just out of reach just above, climbing into shadow. Have you ever thought?

We lean against the boulders 14,000 feet closer to

God, heaven, and our words dance like tongues. I
open my journal and write them down, our words.

Her lips behind my ear, whisper, Be still, don't
speak.

Her brow wrinkles in concentration, her arms
hold me close, and we watch the red lipstick tip rise
from the smooth gold tube between her fingers, the
bathroom mirror beyond, doubling. Be still.

Her breasts press into my shoulder blades, her
hair whispers around my neck. Be still, don't speak.
She paints my mouth, hers.

The next morning, I leave her in my bed, her
body light in the darkness, the morning air damp
with the smells of hay and animals. *I am without
time.*

I write in red lipstick on my mirror. I love you.

revelation

*It is the beginning and the end. She is the word:
tongue, kiss, breast, thigh, heaven, air, water, land,
animal, woman, love.*

*I hear myself moaning in some other time, in this
time, in all time.*

Oh god.

Oh god.

*Oh god. She touches my hands, unfolds them to
see what is written there. She reads my palms with
her tongue. I feel my time line curl in on itself in her
warm breath. My hands remain open, aching, and
wet.*

She lifts her chin, and my mouth is sucked into

the shadow of her collarbone. I taste her pulse, open the skin to that warm animal with my teeth. I hear her groan, mine, released from some dark light place within.

She opens my shirt, buttons flying into a void, cloth disintegrating into dust, and my nipples are hard, hungry for her taste. She laps at them, pilings in a foggy lake.

She inhales my fingers into fire, water, darkness, light. I am baptized, my nerves tingling on her tongue.

She opens me with her red mouth, her thigh, her long soft hand. I am sand, sucking her in. She rocks with my hips, her shoulders the soft white-gold of the moon, hair spread out like a jellyfish across my thighs, her bare back between my knees.

She is wide open for me, and I drink in a new light, breathe deep the thin air of heaven, touch something true with my tongue, hard and soft, slower and faster. Trilling a new word.

Seals are broken. Skin has evaporated. She is creating me in some other plane. I am creating her.

The shutters are wide: light, shadow, all the images overlap, layer.

Music, swamp, animal. Word. Oh God.

I am coming for the first time, the last time, all time. Beginning. Ending. And all things are new.

To Approach the East
Kathleen Collins

I circle the space of all the women I have ever loved and lost — that I may open a new circle in my life, the circle of discovery of a new love.

My fourth-grade teacher. Dark and swift, unmarried, tall, lean. I remember my seat by the window, my looking up toward her by the board.

The sixth-grade teacher. Frightening but with power in her eye that riveted and excited me. I never had her for class, but I had her for choral reading at Christmas time.

The gym teacher in junior high. I yearned for her. I scanned every street and lot for her car as I walked by. She gave me rides home after softball games, and I coveted her children's places with all my heart.

The older girl in Rainbow Girls to whom I wrote. My mother's cousin had told me I should join and that she would pay for the necessary gown. I was entitled because my grandfather was a Mason, and not only a Mason, but the highest order of Mason.

I called her Auntie Eunice. In my family, any adult friend was called *aunt* or *uncle,* and I was halfway grown up before I figured out that lots of them had no blood connection to us at all. After that insight I began to deliberately drop the honorary title from those I didn't like. Auntie Eunice retained her title. She was a heavy woman, solid as a mountain. She spoke with a brusque authority I liked and feared. She came and went alone in her own car.

Auntie Eunice was a major force in Eastern Star and had connections. Once I saw them on their way to Star: they wore evening gowns and perfume and jewelry that glittered. They carried sparkling velvet evening bags and closed themselves into the car with only women's voices talking a quintet. She made sure I was invited into Rainbow Girls. Then she readied me. She took me to the beauty parlor for the first time. They gave me a permanent. I sat in the thick odors of the mirrors and shrank but watched the change from the sausage curls my mother had given me the year before.

When I was little, Auntie Eunice had taken me to her office in the city and kept me there all day. I was scared, but I watched everything that happened.

She sat me at her big desk, gave me paper and pens and pencils, and told me to use the phone. We'd never had a phone, and I didn't know how to use it. I watched her. She took me with her from room to room as she told people what to do or listened to what they said. I didn't understand what they talked about. But I did understand that when Auntie Eunice ordered, men obeyed. It would never have occurred to me to refuse to go into the Rainbow Girls.

In my first formal, wearing just a touch of lipstick and some new perfume, I went through my initiation of candlelight and speeches, flowers and little programs with tassels like at a dance. It was beautiful and safe and more fun than a dance: There were only girls. A little scared, but pleased, I listened and I watched.

Almost right away I was appointed Keeper of the Paraphernalia. I never found out what the paraphernalia was because the Sister of Patriotism got sick and they advanced me to fill the vacancy. I liked that. I got to sit in the Bow, which was in the center of the room, and I was as nationalistic as the next. My brothers were away in the Pacific fighting the Japanese, and my father had fought in World War I. The next year they made me Sister of Religion. That presented me with a dilemma because I believed in very abstract sorts of things like beauty and truth, love and nature, and had seldom gone to church.

I was no hypocrite. I lay awake at night trying to translate the religious meaning of the speech I gave

each new initiate into ideas of beauty and truth. *God,*
I thought, means many things to many people, and
these lines can be interpreted many ways. I ascribed
my own meaning to every line and spoke my piece
with reverence and a fervor I connected with nature
and love, Shakespeare and Millay.

My friend Sandy and I discussed the ethics of this
as we walked home from school. She thought it could
be taken any way you wanted and that whatever any
new girl made of it, that was fine. She and I also
discussed who would go to every meeting. I always
went. It had never occurred to me before not to go.
I'd invited Sandy to join and felt responsible for her,
but she seldom attended. She lived in an apartment
building by the lake. She was in love with a man
who lived in a downstairs apart- ment. He was forty.
She was then fifteen. Those late Saturday night
excuses were too good not to use: She spent that
time in bed with him, and it worried me. We walked
the streets after school, debating whether he would
ever marry her. I thought she should go to college.
She thought her father would kill both of them if
they got caught. I found it interesting that she liked
making love. I worried about her lies because I
believed in truth. I also believed in love.

The three who held the highest offices in Rainbow
Girls — Worthy Advisor, Associate Worthy Advisor,
and Sister of Charity — were friends. The Sister of
Faith was not in their circle, and the Sister of Hope
was a hard-working girl, utterly lacking in glamor,
who had been elected to the hierarchy out of a kind
of group obligation. These three were a tight knot
until the Sister of Charity had to resign when the
rumor behind the whispers finally became a visible

fact. There were stories of her running away with the sailor who made her pregnant as well as stories of her coming home, and I never knew the truth. That left the other two, and I wanted to join them. But by then I was older and had found friends in high school who teased me incessantly about going to Rainbow Girls. They knew about politics and an Italian film with subtitles called *Bicycle Thief,* and I followed them around. Though they could not understand and mocked and laughed, I still went to Rainbow Girls.

It was the Worthy Advisor that I loved. Her name was Lou. She hung out all the time with the Associate, Shireen. Shireen was a silly, sweet sort of girl who looked like June Allyson, and I couldn't believe that Lou could really see anything in Shireen. Lou looked like Maureen O'Hara and spoke in a deep and steady voice, and she had dark brown eyes and hands that held the steering wheel as steady as Hepburn the rudder of the African Queen. After the meetings were over, the younger elect got to tag along when they went for hamburgers and milkshakes. Lou had a car. She drove us home.

I prayed weekly that she would take everyone else home first. I dreamed of being alone in the car with her. I didn't have any idea of what we would say, let alone do, if that dream came true. But I shivered and hoped, and my heart pounded week after week.

I began to write letters to Lou. At first I didn't send them. I had given her presents when she was elected to office and I had put little notes on the presents every time and signed them *Love.* She had even given me a token gift, which I knew was protocol, when she was installed. I carried the card

deep in my pocket: It was signed, *Affectionately, Lou.*
I began to write long letters to her, letters of
appreciation for her work, her dedication, her
wonderful qualities as a leader, as a person, as
herself.

I cannot remember now, nearly fifty years later,
what I said. I can remember with great clarity, however, how I felt. I can remember writing and re-
writing in my room at night, folding the letter in the
envelope, addressing it, shredding it. And I can
remember finally sending one and waiting, heart
thumping, hands sweating, until Lou flung a perfectly
decent verbal reply to me as we walked toward the
car after the next meeting. Lou damned with faint
affection my profound love, saying something like,
"Thanks for the letter. It's nice to know people think
I'm doing a good job."

During the initiation meetings that seemed to
happen often, we all dressed up in formal evening
gowns. It seemed to me the highest officers all wore
beautiful colored gowns, and we in the Bow wore
only white with ribbons for the colors of our station.
I loved the semicircle in the center of the room,
loved the poetry of our colors. Red, orange, yellow,
green, blue, indigo, and violet. I liked patriotism's
color better than religion's. I think patriotism was
blue, but perhaps it was indigo; religion was certainly
orange. I would have preferred to be the Sister of
Love: red. First in the Bow and more important, in
my opinion, than almost anything. Although I was
big on Hope and Charity as well — I considered
Charity to be love as in the passage in Corinthians,
"And now abideth faith, hope, and charity, these

three; but the greatest of these is charity." I'd heard
a sermon once on love and charity being the same if
you took into account the true and deep meanings in
life. I liked and believed that.

So I sat in my chair in the Bow and was two-
thirds of the way up the long room toward Lou, the
Worthy Advisor, who sat on her throne. Anyone
wanting to speak had to ask, "May I approach the
East?" and Lou had to answer them. She always said
yes. There was a sort of desk to the right of her,
and the Treasurer sat there. She was a sad girl who
had been elected treasurer twice and would never be
elected Sister of Faith, which started one on the
ascendant route to Worthy Advisor. I knew she
wouldn't, though I didn't know why. There were
many things like that in Rainbow Girls, that one
knew but didn't know why, such as the Investigation
Committees that verified a number of things when
they visited some applicant for membership. Exactly
what it was we went to verify I doubt that anyone
other than the Mother Advisor even knew. Perhaps
money mattered, perhaps the decor of the living
room? I had a feeling that Sandy had just barely
made it in. I knew if they caught her in her old man
lover's bed she would be out forever. Everyone
viewed the Sister of Charity's pregnancy as high
tragedy, but it was considered the tragedy of young
love. Sandy's would be considered deceit and crude
sex, not romantic love. I knew that.

Anyway, I sat there in the Bow and watched as
others made their speeches, lit their candles, reported
on their sales of cards for the Christmas drive or the
plans to go carol at the old folks home. I signed up

to go, even though I couldn't carry any kind of tune, because Lou would drive a car there. And I knew if I was lucky, I could maneuver to be a passenger in that car. And it was a long drive.

I watched Lou and Shireen laughing together and knew that I shouldn't do it, but eventually I wrote another letter to Lou. It was a love letter. I knew it was and I thought it wasn't. I knew it was because of how I felt. I thought it wasn't because we were both girls, and girls couldn't be in love with one another. On balance I decided in the interest of a lifetime friendship I should send it. I told her that I loved her and quoted the lines from Whittier's *Maud Muller,* "For of all sad things of tongue or pen, the saddest are these: 'It might have been!' " That was to explain how urgent it was that I ask her to be close friends, how deeply I wanted to be her closest friend. I asked her to burn the letter after she had read it.

Then I waited. When we went out after the meetings were over, when all the girls in their long gowns with their pretty little evening bags piled into the cars with the girls who were old enough to drive and whose parents let them use the car or the one or two who had their own cars, I got in Lou's car. I always sat in the right-hand corner of the backseat because then I could see her face, sideways, better than from any other place. I didn't have enough status to ride in front. Shireen rode in front. They were, after all, the same age, and held the highest offices, and if the Sister of Charity hadn't fallen from grace, she, too, would have been riding there.

From the backseat I couldn't hear every word. I could hear some, guess at others, and only shiver and pray that the secret looks and laughs weren't about me.

We parked in the lot of the local drive-in. In the '40s that was adventurous living. I had been to Bartel's for milkshakes. I had seen bad boys sneaking cigarettes outside the school on their way home, and I had even heard about boys drinking beer. When the cars full of girls in long gowns pulled away from the meeting hall where we held our meetings, said our inspirational pieces, admired one another's necklaces and clip-on earrings (no one yet had pierced their ears), we went to the drive-in for milkshakes and hamburgers. Sometimes we stayed there, talking, until late, or pulled over in front of one of our houses and just sat, talking, while the worst among us sneaked a cigarette, always talking, until long into the night.

For me the wild part of the evening was inside my heart. It was almost enough to be in the presence of Lou Browne. Not quite enough. That's why I wrote the letter. I wanted to be part of the front seat crowd. I wanted to be counted in. I wanted to get phone calls from Lou. I wanted to know the very latest news about the Sister of Charity's marriage or lack thereof, what she said, what he said, when he shipped out, where she would live when the baby came. Most of all I wanted to be the last one taken home.

And one night I was. Lou pulled up to my house and stopped the car. There was no one else with her. She hadn't said anything yet about the letter. She hadn't written back. I didn't have any slip of paper to carry in my pocket, to memorize again and again, to check against the memorized words inscribed deep in my heart. I could barely breathe, being where I had dreamed of being, alone with Lou in the dark, my eyes on her as they always were and hers about to turn on me.

She was kind. She told me we were friends but that she was older, had close friends already. She thanked me for the letter. She told me she would do exactly what I had said to do; she took it out of her pocket, got out of the car, scrunched it on the concrete and lit it with a match from her other pocket. I could not look at Lou, crouched in the street in front of her parked car. I watched the paper curl and shrivel, the sheets darken, drift into themselves, crumble, the black ash dissolve, melt into itself, disappear inward until there was nothing left but a blackened mark on the grey concrete. She got back in the car, turned to me and said that she thanked me, that she would remember.

Ten years later, after I had gone away to college, married, given birth, and returned to my native city, I saw Lou Browne. I was walking, pushing my baby in a stroller, my three-year-old by my side. I saw Lou and Shireen still walking together, still laughing together directly across the street from me. I knew Shireen was married by then, but I didn't know about Lou Browne. My breathing tightened.

I wanted to cross the street, introduce myself, show them my children, tell them about my husband, about my writing. I wanted to show them both what a great success I was. I wanted to fully counteract any laughing about me that they had ever done. I wanted to see Lou Browne once more.

I didn't cross the street. And it was another fifteen years before I fell in love with a woman who loved me and I discovered that I would walk on the lesbian side of the street forever after that. And did and am wonderfully happy doing so.

I remember Rainbow Girls and the candlelight and the girl at the door keeping strangers out. I remember hearing, "May I approach the East?" and Lou nodding and allowing someone to draw nigh. I remember wishing she would take me home last after our milkshakes. I remember her voice after she burned my letter, saying she would remember.

Thanksgiving 1958

Susan   Johnson

My mother tells me that Beth and I knew each
other when we were five-year-olds in kindergarten
together. I wish I had fallen in love with her then,
but I confess to having no memory of her preschool
self. Not until I was eighteen did I fall in love with
Beth, but then my adoration was complete. I was in
love the way teenagers are in love: obsessively,
chaotically, passionately, and — if you were a baby
lesbian in the nineteen fifties — totally unconsciously.

At the time, I understood nothing of homosexuality as a condition, nothing of the underground culture of gay women, nothing of my own sexuality. I simply wanted to be in Beth's presence. I wanted to be in her presence all the time. A popular song, "To Know, Know, Know You," expressed exactly how I felt. When I was with Beth I was completely, ecstatically happy. I soared.

I remember sitting next to her on the plaid davenport in her family's living room while she read me stories from *Winnie the Pooh,* tales that — because *she* read and loved them — I found poignant and funny and deeply profound. After a story or two I would swing my legs up and stretch out with my head in her lap while she read on. I was blissful. Her mom would come down from upstairs with sewing in her hands, "Aren't you two girls sweet," she'd say.

When not with Beth I was earthbound again, just a regular high-school girl. I studied Latin and chemistry; I edited the high-school paper; I went to the Unitarian Church with my family; I pretended an interest in which boy took me to the Autumn Leaves fall dance. But my whole being was alert for the ring of the phone: Perhaps I would be saved. Perhaps I would be born again.

Sometime during the summer between high school and college, I had a premonition. I was alone on the screened-in back porch of my family's home. The air was warm and humid, scented with the roses from my grandmother's garden. I felt private and safe and virtuous, laboring through all 932 pages of *Anna Karenina.* I remember looking up from the page, staring into space, and — with that blatant egotism and innocent wonderment that only adolescents can

achieve — thinking, "Here I am, good looking, smart,
successful, well liked, destined for a great life. I
wonder what is going to alter this picture?"

After Beth and I graduated we went to separate
colleges, in part at the urging of parents who wanted
us not to be "too dependent" on each other. I saw
Beth next at a football weekend where we were
ostensibly the dates of two boys from home. I was
carrying on desultory chitchat with my host about
fall semester classes when I heard her voice echoing
down the dormitory corridor. "Suzie," she called.
"Where are you?" From that moment I was awash in
feelings so intense I was nauseous. I was too excited
to eat, too distracted to make coherent conversation.
(One of the boys had been known to say I was the
most intelligent person he knew whom he'd never
heard say an intelligent thing.) I was too happy to be
careful. I could only drink beer and giggle, which is
what Beth and I did all weekend.

The boys had arranged for us to stay in a
rooming house where we shared the same double bed.
Each night we extricated ourselves from them as
early as we could without being ungracious and made
arrangements to meet the next day as late as we
could without being ill-mannered. I fear we were
both. This churlishness was in aid of spending the
maximum possible time alone together. We devoted
these priceless private hours to talking and giggling,
wrestling and giggling, and rubbing backs and
giggling. I remember cool white sheets and flowered
pillowcases and matching wallpaper and bedspreads,
something with violets. There was a lot of tickling,
too. But, while we may have been acting like

children, for the first time we were together as
adults. We were out in the big world, able to choose
for ourselves. And we were choosing each other.

The weekend ended and we parted, but with a
plan to meet for Thanksgiving weekend in New York
City, a destination close to both our colleges.

Thanksgiving weekend closely resembled the
football weekend in many particulars. We had companions, this time two girlfriends from home, but
again Beth and I had a hotel room to ourselves. We
tried to get as much time alone together as we could,
but we also took in some sights, including a drag
show in Greenwich Village. Over many gin and
tonics, elbows on the tiny tables, we wrinkled our
brows trying to figure out what felt different about
these performers we were watching. On the way back
to the hotel in our cab, we compared notes enough to
figure out the gender complexities of what we'd seen.
I was a bit shocked.

The first night Beth and I took up where we'd
left off, talking and wrestling and back-rubbing and
giggling. Then we passed out. We awoke to a terrific
racket outside, stumbled to our window, and were
startled to see a giant Mickey Mouse pitching and
bobbing directly outside. Bands played and ticker tape
fell. It was the annual Macy's Thanksgiving Day
parade. In our agitated and hungover state, the whole
scene seemed surreal. We also thought it was
hilarious.

Somehow the day passed, and again Beth and I
were alone in our room. The hotel had given us twin
beds and — after some joking and kidding around —
we fell asleep, snuggled up to each other in the same
bed. By the next morning the emotional terrain had

changed. The scene was so charged that — thirty-seven years later — I grow breathless remembering it. We had both awakened, gotten up for a few moments, and returned to the same small bed, rumpled with the night's sleep. Beth was stretched out on her back, and I was lying on my side next to her, my left elbow bent, holding up my head. With my right hand I traced the contours of her face. We were both in pajamas, but we had stopped giggling. There was a hush in the room, a sense of time suspended.

My fingers traced along her jaw, across her cheekbones, above her eyebrows. I repeated the pattern, slowly, calmly, but this time after each touch I leaned over and gently kissed the place my fingers had just left. Then, with complete deliberation, knowing full well where I was headed, I brushed her lips with my fingers and, with just the slightest pause, kissed her lips.

The kiss was soft and brief, but it had changed everything. Beth didn't respond, but she didn't withdraw either, and I lay back next to her, exhausted with what I had risked.

My memory ends there. I suppose we got up and went to meet our friends. I know we didn't become lovers that weekend. But we did soon become lovers, and for three years we were each other's sweethearts.

Beth gradually drifted away from me and married after our college graduation. We are now distant friends. I became and have remained a lesbian and know it was through loving Beth and desiring her that I learned I was capable of passionate love.

Now, nearly forty years later, I look back on that Thanksgiving scene and wonder what happened to impel me toward that kiss. I know at the time I used alcohol to deny — and help me along — the dangerous path of my growing attraction for women; that morning I was sober. I had been loving Beth within the constrictions of both our well-meaning families; that morning we were anonymous and alone in New York City. I had been socialized to think that, with the exception of myself, men were men and women were women; the drag show publicly called that tidy duality into question — and, no doubt, adolescent hormones had something to do with it.

But while all these factors satisfy my mind, only one explanation lives in my heart: I believe I was simply inspired.

One Detail Glaringly Lacking

Penny Hayes

She had known him for twenty-five good years,
years filled with devotion and the pleasant safeness of
a strong marriage. He had just gotten out of the
Marines when they'd first met. He was twenty-one,
she, nineteen. She knew from the start that he was
the man she would live with for the rest of her life.
He said she looked exactly as he'd dreamed all his
life: small-boned, slender, black hair curling around

her ears and neck, green Irish eyes laughing even during hard times. She said he was full of baloney.

Working as a forest ranger, he spent a lot of time hiking the state's hundreds of miles of northern mountain trails, checking out people and their camping equipment, making sure they were traveling safely. He always returned by nightfall.

She stayed home mostly, in her tiny town of fifteen hundred folks or so, puttering around their small, single-story dwelling, planting flowers, mowing the yard, visiting family and friends.

Although it went in spurts, they had a very contented love life. Sometimes weeks would pass without much more occurring between them than their holding each other. At other times, they enjoyed each other's bodies for several evenings in a row, attaining satisfying climaxes and falling asleep relaxed and peaceful. She was sure she had the best life could offer: a loving husband, relatives close by, several friends with whom she had gone to school and visited still.

Then he had been transferred to an incredibly liberal college town of forty-five thousand, full of robust students, unusual shops, and busy, oversized malls. It was a town about which she knew nothing in a location she had never before seen and, she reflected, too far from loved ones. During their unsettling move, only her husband and her little dog had remained constant.

She began to be afraid when he left for work as a ranger in the southernmost part of the park's mountains. As the years passed, she stayed more and more inside the house, the only place where she felt almost completely safe. The job of growing any flowers eventually fell to her husband, as did caring for the lawn and, finally, shopping for groceries. In the last few years, even walking to the mailbox not a tenth of a mile down the drive had become a frightening challenge. She had tried driving the Jeep but found herself unable to venture twenty feet from the garage without experiencing an overwhelming sense of dread. Only going for walks with him by her side, her hand gripping his, was bearable. Were she asked about her life, she would readily assure the questioner that everything was fine. Yet, she was continually fitful.

Her husband talked to her, consoled her, and performed special little things for her like fetching morning coffee to her in bed and bringing home comedy videos to vitalize her spirits. He stayed home as much as his job allowed, and when he had to travel overnight, he frequently telephoned, while she lived in undeviating fear that he might never return.

The unexplainable trepidation continued to engulf her. She eventually began counseling, her husband driving her to the therapist's once each week. There, she struggled to fathom her innermost being. Weeks of psychotherapy stretched into months, and months into years. Nothing seemed to change.

One day she could stand it no longer. As she glanced at the *Goings-On* in that evening's newspaper, she read again an ad she had been following for months. "There's a women's support group in this town," she said. "I'd like to go see what it's about." Fighting waves of nausea, she insisted she would drive herself.

He was encouraged by her extraordinary willingness to leave the house without his having to pressure her into doing so, something he'd had to do for years. The evening of the meeting, he walked her to the car door, kissed her, and promised several times he would be right there when she got back.

In half an hour she returned, unable to find the address. The city was too large, the night too dark. She *hated* driving in the dark. She hated driving.

"Give it one more try," he urged, his deep, watchful eyes calming her, his shock of graying hair tousled as usual, his large size giving her a sense of security as his six-foot height towered over her five.

She was crying hard now. "I can't," she wailed. "I can't *do* it. I'm afraid."

He took her in his arms and held her close. "You can, honey. Please try one more time. If you don't find the place this time, then I'll take you."

With her slender fingers locked in a death grip around the Jeep's steering wheel, she drove uncomfortably hunched over. Her eyes were wide and staring, dry from lack of blinking in her apprehension that she might miss a street sign, drive the wrong way down a one-way street, hit a car — or, God forbid, a person. She could feel her body occasionally twitching as her consternation increased and her heart pounded erratically. Forty-five appalling minutes later, she reached her destination.

She peeled her cramped hands from the wheel and stepped from the vehicle. Making her way into the building, she dabbed at a glistening sheen of sweat coating her face. Feeling the dread of a magnitude that nearly buckled her knees, she approached the front desk and whispered to the pretty, young receptionist, "I'm looking for the women's support group."

Pointing to her left, the smiling woman said, "That door over there."

She forced herself to walk into the room.

Inside was a large circle of chairs seating twenty-five or so women of varying sizes and ages. "I'm sorry I'm late." Again a whisper, but she had gotten the words out. She had also found the place and she had found the group. Momentous accomplishments, she judged as she sank into the nearest chair.

The women talked; she listened — and looked. There was a variety of reasons for people having come that night, some plainly dissatisfied with their lives, others wanting to stop smoking, hoping that talking with the group might help. A few, like her, were fearful of the unknown no matter how exciting it might be. Jobs were discussed, women complaining that they were unrecognized and underpaid. Several had come just to enjoy the camaraderie of women supporting women. They were clothed in everything from sweatshirts and jeans to professional attire. She was glad she was in a modest blouse and slacks.

One of the women was a lesbian. She'd never seen a lesbian before. Who would have guessed such a thing? The woman was quite stunning, dressed in a flaring green dress, heels, and jewelry. Her makeup was meticulously worn, her blond hair a series of waves down her back. Several others said that they, too, were lesbians although they were not nearly so pretty nor as decked out.

As the evening grew late, she listened to an array of stories regarding home life and loss of family members, or pets, which the lesbians seemed to believe were family members. Mentioned, too, was the inability to express oneself to her husband, boyfriend, or girlfriend and an ineptitude at handling money. Somebody mentioned condoms, their value and their interference. The gathering's candidness astonished her.

She went to the affair three weeks in a row, later examining everything she had heard with her counselor. Without her realizing it, she discussed lesbianism a greater percentage of the time. She thought "them" strange but cute and wondered how they came to be "that" way.

It was during the seventh meeting that she changed — toward men, toward women, toward herself — making her wonder where the hell her head had been for the past forty-three years.

Entering the room, she shyly addressed several ladies while noticing the usual spattering of new faces.

Perhaps a half hour had passed when, sitting opposite her, a newcomer caught her ear with a lilting voice while speaking of family issues involving an older son.

As the continuing sound of the woman's voice bathed her with visions of a rising sun, a boiling ocean, a look into a part of herself she had never before seen, a baffling fullness settled in her breast. She took a deep breath and felt as though the old family mule had kicked her dead center of her chest just as the ornery old beast had done when she was twelve or so. The jolt was unpleasant, terribly unpleasant. She fought it, fought against it, fought with it. By the end of the meeting she wanted only to get out of there.

She went to counseling and during the next

several sessions probed further into lesbianism, what it was, how it felt, why some women were lesbians and some were not. "How does one determine one's sexual identity?" she asked.

"You just know," the adviser explicitly summarized.

That day she left the office shaken, convinced her therapist was a lesbian. How else could she know so much, give such precise answers?

And now, she decided, she herself was probably one of *those.* As if she wasn't already dealing with enough of life's challenges. Whatever would she tell her husband? What would his response be? Would he still love her? Shun her? Beat her?

She didn't mention a word to him. Instead, she chose to ignore her newfound self and encouraged mad sex with him for the next six weeks, laughing, acting unusually aggressive — and not attending any more meetings or going to counseling.

Thirty-one climaxes later (she'd kept close track), she knew, *knew,* something was missing in her life. Everything was still the same between them. Everything, just as it had always been, but she was now clear that there was one detail glaringly lacking. She hadn't an inkling of what it was, only that it was absent.

She returned to the women's meetings, never talking, never asking questions, listening most intently to the lesbians, women she didn't understand, had not come in contact with before coming to this group, was a bit frightened of.

In the end, she felt she must tell her husband. His reaction stunned her. He broke down in tears. They then worked together to give her that elusive component. They didn't achieve it. Eventually she moved out of their bedroom and then out of their home, feeling that to sleep with and live with him was dishonorable. Unable to shake her resolution, he had to let her go.

Six months later she went to bed with a woman to whom she had become recklessly attached and who said to her, "Touch me here, and here, and here."

She did, hypnotized by her lover's intimate and intricate anatomy. She wallowed in the softness of her full breasts, savored the flatness of her lover's pelvic region, her deepest, innermost parts laden with heat and wetness. Reaching a searing climax, her disciple nearly threw them both off the bed.

Then she heard, "And now you, my young lesbian."

Young? She was several years the woman's senior — but not by this experience. Something unendurable let loose of her mind, and she knew she could do anything, go anywhere. She was unequivocally fearless.

Fiery lips came down upon her own, quickening her heart. Naked skin pressed against hers, continuously rising excitement causing perspiration to course down her sides. She felt her rib cage bend beneath her lover who rested upon her and weighed a good twenty pounds more than she, and all of it satiny muscle.

Her nipples stood rigidly upright, aching painfully in anticipation of those perfectly shaped lips and pearly white teeth about to explore them. Down they came sucking, nibbling, with tongue wet as egg white. Down they dipped to the end of her sternum, past

her navel to the bridge of her pelvis, into her thick
hair and then — into her chasm.

She could picture those lips as she heard her own
ponderous breathing and that of her lover. She
discerned the eagerness of the exploring mouth, felt
the strength rippling across broad shoulders. Hands
as strong as steel and tender as a babe grasped her
inner thighs, lifted her knees, and spread her legs.
Fluid emanated from deep within her.

"You fill my mouth with your heart," her lover
said.

Well, the buildup had certainly been notably
different, but the completion was much like those
she'd experienced with her husband. She supposed
she could now relax.

Unanticipated, her lover touched her in a new
place. A second undeniably different kind of climax
burst upon her, paralyzing her brain and deadening
her ability to do anything but feel unquenchable love
for this exquisite woman. Her head rolled from side
to side. As she breathed, she inhaled so deeply her
voice became ragged. Her throat burned painfully.
Tears fell like violent rainstorms as unidentifiable
sensations swept her away. Her knees were pressed
against her chest, the woman between her legs
continuing to do *something* to her. Her tongue. Her
tongue!

She laughed and cried until she collapsed. Spent,
she would never, ever move again. Her tears
continued as her breathing returned to normal and
her heart slowed a degree. A loud ringing in her ears
gradually receded while she clutched her lover to her
breast.

The following morning while confidently driving back to her apartment, she understood what had been missing between her and her husband: passion. Passion! She thought she'd had it all with him. Everything! She had had love certainly, but never before had she experienced passion.

It's all in the head, then, she contemplated while waiting for a light change. The body does nothing but follow.

She hoped that one day her husband would remarry, enjoy such passion with someone who could return the same ardor to him. She never had, yet felt that all their lives she had cheated him. She would have to learn to deal with that one.

In the meantime, she laid plans for an entirely different lifestyle from the one she'd lived for the past twenty-five years. As she pulled into her garage, a smile split her face as though she were, once again, a small child experiencing her first big-top circus.

Always a Bridesmaid

Peggy J. Herring

Rosalie was spending Christmas day with Arty and his parents the first time she met Trina. The three LaRues had been acting a little strange all afternoon, but it wasn't anything Rosalie could really put her finger on. A ringing telephone or a neighbor's car door slamming seemed to send them into a nervous frenzy, and no one could pass up a window without parting the drapes and checking down the street.

"What's the matter with everybody today?" she whispered as Arty handed her a cup of eggnog.

"Nothin'." He kept peeking around the corner to make sure neither of his parents could hear them.

An hour later there was a sharp knock on the front door.

"Don't answer it," Mrs. LaRue hissed.

The next round of knocks was much louder, and followed by, "Open up! It's Christmas, goddamn it!"

Rosalie was startled to see Mr. LaRue spring from his chair and charge the door. All eyes were locked on the foyer as Trina came in loaded down with presents. She set them on the floor near the Christmas tree, and Rosalie's eyes went directly to the NOBODY KNOWS I'M A LESBIAN printed in bold letters across her T-shirt. Rosalie smiled and then felt a jolt when Trina looked over at her.

"You must be Arty's fiancée," Trina said, her voice low and husky. "I've heard about you from other family members."

"Oh?" Rosalie said. She was a bit embarrassed at not knowing anything about this stranger. "And you are?"

Trina chuckled. "Arty's little sister. Trina LaRue. This is my annual ten-minute visit. It's nice to meet you."

Rosalie shot a questioning look over in Arty's direction. They'd been dating for almost a year, and he had never mentioned anything about a sister before.

"I've brought presents," Trina said cheerfully. "Even for you, Rosalie. Now don't everyone rush over here at once."

Rosalie didn't have a chance to respond because all hell broke loose right about then. Mr. LaRue picked up his present, opened the door, and pitched it out in the front yard. Mrs. LaRue and Arty, like two windup toy soldiers, did the same. All four of the LaRues — Arty, Trina, and both of their parents — stood with arms crossed looking at Rosalie, waiting for her to do something. The pressure was tremendous, and Rosalie could feel cool sweat beginning to pop out on her forehead.

Finally Trina leaned closer and nodded toward the remaining present. "Need help with that? Want me to throw it out for you?"

Rosalie reached over and picked it up, eyeing them all suspiciously. "Are you people nuts?"

Trina threw her head back and laughed. "I know you like me to keep my visits short, so I'll be on my way. Merry Christmas to all. It's been fun as usual." To Rosalie she nodded and tossed that mane of chestnut-colored hair away from her face. "You might wanna think about this marriage thing a little more. You can do better, you know."

Once Trina was out the door, Mr. LaRue turned the television on, while Mrs. LaRue cried all the way to the kitchen. In the meantime, Rosalie managed to yank Arty aside to get the scoop on his sister. The LaRues had kicked Trina out ten years earlier when she was still in high school. That had happened after she told them she was gay.

"She moved to Dallas," Arty said. "Shows up on Christmas every year and stays just long enough to make us crazy."

Rosalie was flabbergasted. "She drives for five

hours and stays for two minutes every Christmas? That's it?"

Arty shrugged. "Yeah. That's it. She hauls in some presents and then we throw them out the door. We yell at each other for a while and then she leaves. It's like a fuckin' tradition, okay?"

Rosalie was absolutely appalled by the whole thing, and she noticed that neither Trina nor the present-tossing incident were mentioned again the rest of the day. Rosalie, however, kept reliving that eye-contact-induced jolt Trina had given her when she first walked in.

The following afternoon Rosalie got Trina's number from directory assistance and called to thank her for the present. Over the next several weeks the two spoke quite often. Rosalie had it in the back of her mind that she wanted to help put the family back together again. She informed Arty that she wanted Trina included in the wedding.

"Included how?" he asked.

"I want her to be a bridesmaid."

From there they proceeded to have their first big fight. They argued all the way across town and were still going at it when they pulled into the LaRues' driveway.

"That queer's not welcome here," Mr. LaRue stated flatly after Arty told him what Rosalie had in mind. "I'll see to it they won't even let her in the church!"

Rosalie elbowed her future husband and simply said, "Please remind him again who's paying for this."

She called Trina later the next day and convinced

her to be in the wedding. "You realize, of course, that my parents might not go if I'm there."

"Sure, they'll go," Rosalie said confidently.

During the next few weeks, Rosalie recalled bits and pieces of numerous conversations she and Trina had. Her stories about life with the LaRues were entertaining. At one point Trina confessed to accusing her father of naming her after a stripper he used to know. "He denied it much too loudly, if you ask me. Much too loudly." Her laughter was contagious. "Trina LaRue," she said with a touch of drama. "Just saying it makes me wanna take my clothes off."

Rosalie could stay on the phone with her for hours; she thought about calling her at least three or four times a day. She kept remembering Christmas and Trina's drop-dead gorgeous body bending to set those presents down. Rosalie didn't place any real significance on that — a nice body is a nice body no matter who it belongs to. Right?

Rosalie also remembered the first time she had touched that body. Trina had arrived from Dallas for an appointment with the dressmaker. Rosalie answered the door and immediately looked at Trina's chest to see what personal message this particular T-shirt would have on it. Trina stood there in the doorway wearing a white open-collar shirt and tight black jeans. She smiled as she caught Rosalie's gaze scrutinizing her breasts and said in that amused, sultry voice, "Like what you see?"

Rosalie blushed all the way to the bone.

Later that same afternoon at the dressmaker's house, Trina picked up a pattern and perused the picture on the front. "Prom dresses," she said.

"Bridesmaids have to wear tacky prom dresses." She eyed the picture a bit more closely. "I think my friend Sebastian wore this in his 'Going to the Chapel' number a few weeks ago."

When the dressmaker had enough of the dress together to seriously begin the fitting, Trina proceeded to take off her shirt, jeans, and soft leather boots without even a hint of shyness. But then with a body like that, Rosalie had noted at the time, who wouldn't want to show it off?

Rosalie could still see Trina standing on a small stool as the dressmaker pinned and hemmed, with Rosalie tugging at the material at Trina's waist to see how much more needed to be taken in. Trina's bare skin felt soft and warm through the gaps in the fabric. The first time Rosalie touched her had been an accident, but the "accidents" seemed to keep happening the rest of the afternoon. At one point Trina glanced down at her from the stool and whispered with that marvelous, husky voice, "Rosalie, babe. Don't tease me like that."

Once again Rosalie had stayed awake all night thinking about her. That little familiar jolt was rapidly turning into something else.

A week later Rosalie found herself on the way to Dallas. She took another sip of lukewarm coffee and made a conscious effort not to think about anything. Leaving San Antonio and seeing Trina again had almost become an emergency. Earlier in the week Rosalie had given Arty his ring back and told her parents she was canceling the wedding. She stopped short of telling them she thought she was a lesbian, however.

She slipped into a phone booth and dialed Trina's number.

"You're here? In Dallas?"

"Yes."

"You and Arty?"

"No. Just me." Rosalie leaned her head against the telephone. "I need to see you."

Trina told her to get in her car and lock the doors. She would be there in twenty minutes.

"Why didn't you let me know you were coming?" Trina asked as she slid into the front seat.

"There wasn't time." Rosalie told her about breaking off the engagement. Trina looked over at her and asked if she was okay. When their eyes met, Rosalie finally recognized that little jolt for what it really was. *You're in love with her, you idiot.*

Trina looked away first and then opened the door. "Follow me. My place isn't too far from here."

Rosalie didn't get nervous until they were climbing the stairs to her apartment. While Trina switched on a few lights and got them something to drink, Rosalie took in the large, tastefully decorated room. A porcelain sculpture of two nude women entwined in an embrace caught her attention on a shelf by the stereo.

"Does Arty know you're here?" Trina sat across from her in the chair next to the sofa. "You two have a fight?"

"This is none of Arty's business." Rosalie took a sip of her drink and then set it down.

"Call him and patch it up," Trina said. She motioned toward a small table near a lamp. "The phone's by the —"

"I think I'm a lesbian."

Trina closed her eyes and rubbed the bridge of her nose. "That's impossible," she said calmly. She set her glass on the table and got up and began to pace. "You had a fight with Arty, and he said some stupid things. Saying stupid things is one of his specialties, by the way, but you'll get used to it. Just give him a call and get it all straightened out."

Rosalie was annoyed at not being taken seriously. Hadn't she been moving in this direction for weeks now? Months possibly? Years maybe? *All your damn life, you dumb shit.*

"I think I'm a lesbian, Trina," she said a little louder.

"You *think* you're a lesbian? Nobody *thinks* she's a lesbian. You either are or you aren't."

"Then I am."

"Like hell you are. Lesbians don't sleep with my brother."

Rosalie was suddenly furious. Her emotions were raw, and she felt like she'd been up for days already. Seeing Trina again should've been the answer to everything, but Rosalie was feeling too foolish at the moment to think clearly. She snatched up her purse and headed for the door.

"Call him," Trina said as she followed her down the hallway. "He's probably worried about you."

"I'm not calling anybody!" Rosalie yanked on the door, but it wouldn't open.

"Where are you going?" Trina said. Her voice was

soft. So soft, in fact, that Rosalie felt a chill race up and down her arms. She turned around and met those searching brown eyes again. "Why did you come here?" Trina whispered.

Rosalie had never been more sure of anything in her life as she stood there. She wanted this woman, and could feel her body responding to her.

"You know why," Rosalie said quietly. She felt weak from the fluttering in her stomach. She reached out slowly and gathered the front of Trina's shirt in her hand and pulled her closer. Rosalie leaned over to kiss her, their lips meeting shyly at first. Trina's tongue touched hers, and a deep, intense, breathtaking kiss followed. A kiss that Rosalie never wanted to end. A kiss that she had waited a lifetime for. A kiss that was over much too quickly.

Rosalie put her arms around Trina's neck; she didn't trust her shaky legs to support her on their own. "Jesus, that was nice," she said dreamily.

Trina's mouth was on her neck and moving along her throat. Rosalie trembled and tightened her arms around her again. She felt the wall suddenly pressing against her back and was grateful to have it there.

No one had ever kissed her that way before, and it was so much better than anything she could have imagined. Trina's mouth was on her ear, gently sucking at the earlobe and then outlining the rest with the tip of her tongue. Rosalie could hear Trina's excitement building as her ragged breath continued grazing the side of her face.

"I should send you on your way," Trina whispered.

Rosalie had no idea what would happen next, but

leaving now certainly wasn't an option. She desperately searched for Trina's mouth again in answer to the suggestion. Trina's hand was under her shirt, causing the most wonderful sensations. After a moment, the hand moved down along Rosalie's ribs and then eased between her legs to rub her through her jeans. Rosalie pulled her mouth away and gasped.

"There's still time to change your mind," Trina said.

"Maybe for you." Rosalie was beyond the point of no return and had Trina in a death grip with her arms still firmly around her neck. The lowering of her zipper was erotic in its own right, but the sound of their mutual heavy breathing was enough to send Rosalie over the edge.

"God, you're so wet," Trina said, the surprise evident in her voice. Her fingers slid through damp curls while her mouth found Rosalie's again. "So wet," Trina murmured.

Rosalie heard something: moaning, slow, deep moaning. As Trina's tongue began to gently probe Rosalie's mouth and match that exquisite stroking between her legs, Rosalie finally recognized the moaning as her own. Trina moved against her so easily, naturally, and Rosalie never wanted the moment to end. That tongue had her at its mercy, and she came with a shudder that saturated her whole body. Rosalie's arms went limp around Trina's neck. Her legs were too shaky to hold her up on their own.

"I've got you," Trina whispered. Her hand stayed in place, and she pressed her body into Rosalie's, keeping her against the wall. Rosalie tightened her arms around Trina's neck once more, not wanting to let go as those wonderful fingers slowly eased out of her.

"Did you get what you came for?" Trina asked.

"Not yet, as a matter of fact." She took Trina's face in her hands and kissed her long and deep, bringing back the tumbling in her stomach. "Show me how to make love to you." Rosalie was touched by the vulnerability she saw in Trina's eyes. It gave her another dash of courage. "Now," Rosalie said. She reached over and began unbuttoning Trina's shirt, remembering how soft her skin had felt that day at the dressmaker's house. Rosalie rubbed her palms over the top of Trina's breasts and whispered, "Show me now, baby."

Trina took her by the hand and led the way to the bedroom. They were all over each other, lips searching while hands roamed easily along cool, sensitive flesh. Rosalie's shirt was pulled over her head just before Trina helped her out of her already unzipped and slightly damp jeans. Rosalie wondered in the back of her mind how lesbians could keep something like this a secret. Why didn't they go door to door spreading the word? Why weren't they handing out pamphlets to female shoppers in the mall?

"You feel so good," Rosalie whimpered. Trina leaned closer and flicked her tongue over a taut nipple. Her warm wet mouth sent surges of pleasure through Rosalie's body as they melted together on the bed.

"Are you doing this to get back at Arty?" Trina asked.

"Arty who?" Rosalie rolled her over on her back and stretched Trina's arms out above her head. "I'm doing this for me." She leaned over and kissed her gently on the mouth. "And you. I want to please you." Trina's murmurs told her more than anything else could have. Rosalie kissed her again and couldn't imagine ever wanting to be anywhere else. "I have no idea what I'm doing, so feel free to jump right in with advice at any time."

Trina closed her eyes and laughed. "You're doing fine." Putting her hands on Rosalie's head, guiding her down to where she needed her the most, was enough to send Rosalie close to the edge again. Rosalie depended on this exercise to give her a starting place, a knowledge base for a future in how to really make love to this woman. She was diligent and thorough in her pursuit of Trina's pleasure. She wanted to show her how much she already cared.

A while later in Trina's arms, Rosalie had more confidence in her newly acquired skills. She had made Trina come with a long, tremulous orgasm, and it amazed her how much more satisfying that had been than tending to her own needs. Trina pushed damp blonde hair away from Rosalie's forehead and kissed her.

"I haven't had a night like this since that softball banquet I got drunk at," Trina said.

"You play softball?"

She shook her head and hugged her. "No. Actually I just make sure I'm always invited to their banquet."

Rosalie nipped at her bare shoulder with a playful bite and curled her fingers to inspect her nails. "How does one get invited to a softball banquet? Sounds like fun."

"One has to hang out with the team after the games, but we won't have time for any of that."

"We won't?" Rosalie tilted her head back as Trina's mouth came to her throat. "No," she agreed with a happy sigh. "I guess we won't."

Laundry Day

Lisa Haddock

Anna was stuck inside her parents' house doing the laundry — her least favorite chore — on a sunny, warm spring afternoon. She could have saved time by going to a self-service laundry, but she was a graduate student. A handful of quarters was a major investment.

She had the house to herself. As they did every weekend, her parents were wandering through a cavernous mall south of town. Never finding what they wanted, complaining about high prices, they always came home empty-handed.

Anna was flipping through the channels on their giant RCA color TV while she waited for the spin cycle to end. Her tiny studio apartment, which was near the university where she was studying, was not wired for cable. Even if it had been, she couldn't afford the monthly fee, and she rarely had the time to watch her small Philco black-and-white set. She was too busy studying for her graduate English classes and teaching two sections of freshman composition.

When they returned from the mall, her parents would pick up where they left off. Her mother would nag her about the impracticality of graduate school, even though her parents weren't paying her tuition and she survived on a meager fellowship and a small loan. Her mother would mutter about Anna's short hair, black biker boots, tattered shorts, and multiple ear piercings — three on the left ear, two on the right. Her father would find an excuse to work in the yard so he wouldn't have to talk to or look at his daughter.

To keep the peace, Anna planned to put on a long-sleeve shirt as soon as she saw her parents' Chrysler sedan in the drive. The shirt would cover her unshaved armpits, her lack of bra, the slogan on her tank top, and her latest outrage — a small tattoo of a rose on her upper arm.

Flicking through the channels, Anna landed on *My Fair Lady*. Rex Harrison was badgering Audrey Hepburn about dropping her *h*'s. She felt a twinge. The movie had been one of Beverly's favorites.

Beverly — a hard-drinking, fun-loving cowgirl —

was a prelaw student who tore through Anna's heart like a tornado out of a greenish-black sky two years back. Anna fell headlong in love; Beverly was mildly entertained. After about six months, Beverly was finished with her bachelor's and Anna. When she headed back to Texas for law school, Anna was left behind to cope with a broken heart and to finish her degree.

Though Anna thought of Beverly less often now, her memory was still painful.

"Shit," she said, turning the set off.

The doorbell rang, and Anna looked up.

The front door was open. There, standing on the front porch, was Jennifer MacIntosh.

"Jenny, what are you doing here?" she said, unlatching the screen door and looking over Jenny, whom she hadn't seen since high school. The passage of five years had made Jenny, a tall woman with deep black eyes and thick black lashes, even more beautiful, Anna thought.

"Lord, you've gone bohemian in a big way," said Jenny, who looked over Anna in astonishment. Jenny wore jeans, pink-and-white running shoes, and a pink Mickey Mouse T-shirt. Anna was dressed for a revolution, with a black DISMEMBER PATRIARCHY tank top, large, ripped denim shorts, black boots, leather bracelets, spiked hair, and unshaved legs and armpits. "Anna, is that a tattoo?"

"Yes, it is," Anna said, feeling more than a little self-conscious.

"Actually, I was looking for your parents. I was driving through the neighborhood. Well, to be honest, I'm having some car trouble," said Jenny, laughing easily and offering a sweet, simple smile.

When Anna saw that expression, the memory returned, sweet and delicate like the scent of honeysuckle on a summer night.

It was the first day of high school. The bell had already rung, and most of the students had already unpacked their instruments. Wearing a light floral sundress, Jenny walked in late and breathless. She quickly apologized to the teacher and took her seat among the violins. She was the most beautiful girl Anna had ever seen.

From the cello section, Anna, amazed, stared at Jenny. Across the room, Jenny caught Anna's eye and offered a sweet, shy smile. Anna looked away, embarrassed.

"Can I use your phone?" Jenny said. "I need to call my husband."

"Husband?" Anna said. Jenny had dated boys throughout high school. Still, her statement produced a surprisingly strong stab of jealousy.

"He's going to be furious at me."

"Mind if I take a look at your car?"

Jenny smiled. "Of course not," she said.

Riding together in Anna's old red Volkswagen, which was plastered with stickers reflecting the driver's politics — radical feminism, lesbian and gay rights, environmentalism, socialism — Jenny directed her friend to the late-model Ford sedan, its blinkers flashing at the side of the road.

Anna tried to start the Ford. It cranked up but wouldn't start. As Anna searched for the hood release, she noticed the gas gauge was pointing to empty.

"Jenny, you're out of gas."

"I'm so glad I didn't call Bill. He would have killed me," she said with an embarrassed laugh.

"Bill Lofton?" Anna said. He was a pasty-faced creep Jenny used to date on and off during high school. Back then, Anna hated his guts, though she didn't understand why. She just knew that he wasn't good enough for her Jenny.

"Yes. That's my hubby. We've been married two years. I would have invited you to the wedding —" Anna raised her hand to cut Jenny off.

After graduation, Jenny went away to a Baptist Bible college in Louisiana. Anna stayed at her parents' house and went to the local university. At first, they wrote each other. Jenny, a devout Baptist, spoke of soul-winning, summer mission work, and Bible seminars. Anna, who had also been raised a Baptist, did her best to shake her religious training as soon as she hit college. A year after high-school graduation, they'd had nothing to say to each other anymore.

"I'm sure there's a gas can out in the garage," Anna said as they pulled into the driveway of her parents' home.

Jenny watched Anna rummage through the garage.

"So, what have you been up to?" Jenny asked. "You still living with your folks?"

"I've got a little studio apartment. I finished my bachelor's in English. Now I'm in my second semester of a master's program in English. It's a women's literature program."

"Like romance novels?" said Jenny.

Anna shrugged. It wasn't worth explaining to her. Jenny had been so well indoctrinated and isolated by the church, she wouldn't know a feminist theory if it came up and bit her on the ass. "What about you?"

"Well, Bill was working on his degree in accounting. He was always so much better at school than I was. So I dropped out after two years. There was no use wasting all that tuition money on me anyway."

At last, Anna found a one-gallon tank behind one of the lawn mowers. "Here it is."

At the gas station, Anna filled the can while Jenny sat in the car. Anna remembered the first time she realized that what she felt for Jenny was stronger than mere friendship, that her indifference to boys might be something more than mere fussiness, self-possession, and budding feminist consciousness.

During their junior year, Jenny and Anna roomed together at the Holiday Inn during a school orchestra trip. Through a mixup in reservations, they wound up with a room to themselves. Most of the other students were sleeping four to a room, two to a bed.

After a late-night concert, Jenny and Anna sat on Anna's bed and watched *Psycho* with the lights off in their room. A few minutes into the movie, Jenny had rested her head on Anna's shoulder. Ever since sophomore year, Anna knew she had a deep affection for Jenny. But she never dreamed they would ever touch. That night, it was happening. Anna wouldn't let herself think about why Jenny was touching her or where it would lead. She simply reacted.

Slowly and tentatively, she put her arm around Jenny, who snuggled closer to her friend. Then, Jenny stretched out across the bed and put her head on Anna's knees. Anna started stroking Jenny's hair. Anna's body tingled with pleasure.

Just then, Janet Leigh was about to be murdered in the shower.

"Oh, I hate this," Jenny said. "Turn it off. Please."

Anna got up and switched off the TV. The room was dark, and Jenny was still stretched out on her bed.

"Can I sleep in your bed tonight?" Jenny asked. "That movie really freaks me out."

"Sure," Anna said, not knowing why her heart was racing.

Anna got under the covers with her back to her best friend. Jenny scooted up behind her, wrapping her arms around her waist.

Every nerve ending in Anna's body tingled. "Jenny," Anna said breathlessly as she turned over. She put her arms around Jenny and brushed her cheek against her friend's. "Oh, Jenny. You don't have to be afraid. It's okay. I won't ever let anything or anyone hurt you."

Jenny pulled her closer. They held each other for a long time. More than anything else, Anna wanted to kiss Jenny. She was slow and careful. She had never kissed anyone before. Not like this, anyway. Anna carefully brushed her lips against Jenny's cheek. Jenny said nothing. Anna kissed her face again. Finally, Anna placed her lips on Jenny's. She felt as if she had been hooked up to an electric current. Jenny's lips parted. Anna, now nearly wild with desire, kissed Jenny more ardently. Then, suddenly, Jenny stiffened and pulled away.

"This is wrong. Besides, we've got to get up early tomorrow," she said. "We've got a concert at nine."

Jenny got up and moved to the other bed, leaving Anna shivering and trembling. She didn't understand what was going on in her body, but she knew she was in love with Jennifer MacIntosh.

She and Jenny never spoke about the incident. They acted as if it never happened. Despite the silence, Anna often dreamed of that night and where it might have led, had Jenny let her go on.

After Anna poured the gas into the tank, Jenny cranked the engine, which started immediately.

She offered a grateful smile. "I can't thank you enough. I'm so lucky you were here. You saved me from getting a big lecture from Bill."

Anna looked into Jenny's face. Jenny laid her hand across Anna's. It was the first time Jenny had touched her since that night. "You don't have to take that from him, you know," Anna said.

"Oh, you'll find out soon enough when you get married," Jenny said.

Anna's heart raced. "Jenny, that's never going to happen —"

Jenny smiled. "Oh, you just wait. You'll find a fellow to change your mind."

"There is no fellow for me, Jenny."

Jenny's face grew troubled, as if she sensed Anna was about to say something frightening. She pulled her hand away. "Look at the time," she said, glancing at her watch. "I'm sorry I have to run like this, but I still have to go to the store and then get home and fix Bill's dinner. Give me a call sometime. We're in the book."

"Hold on," Anna said, not knowing why she was forcing the issue. "Jenny, you're a bright, beautiful woman. You shouldn't let Bill walk on you. You deserve so much more."

"That's nice of you to say," Jenny said, her face confused, her voice tentative.

"I would never treat a woman I loved liked that," Anna said passionately.

Jenny looked down, avoiding Anna's eyes.

"You knew how I felt about you, didn't you?" Anna said softly.

Jenny nodded her head. "I could never be the way you are —"

Anna's temper flared. She was angry at Jenny. Angry at Beverly. Angry at herself for giving herself to women who couldn't or wouldn't give themselves in return. But she didn't say anything.

"I'm sorry," Jenny said, tears beginning to flow.

"Don't be sorry, Jenny," Anna said. "Good-bye." She walked away without looking back.

* * * * *

When Anna returned, her parents were back from the mall.

Her mother met her at the front door. "I thought you went off and forgot your laundry. You are staying for dinner, aren't you?"

"Yes, Mother," she said.

"My God, is that a tattoo?" her mother said, staring at her arm.

"Yes, Mother."

"Where were you?"

"Jenny MacIntosh dropped by. She ran out of gas up the road, so I was helping her out."

"Why didn't you invite her to dinner? She was always such a good influence on you."

Anna shrugged her shoulders. She couldn't put what she was feeling into words. Even if she could, her mother wouldn't want to hear it anyway. She'd made that clear when Anna told her about Beverly. "How was the mall?"

"The prices are out of sight," she said. "And those damned teenagers. There ought to be a law against them."

Anna walked out to the back porch to be alone. Her mother's voice called her back.

"Tell your father to light the grill in about twenty minutes. I'm starting the potatoes now."

Anna nodded at her mother.

Instinct

Diane Salvatore

Leigh waited outside the Cornerstone Cafe, as arranged, at exactly seven. She leaned impatiently against the green, wrought-iron lamppost, her arms folded tightly. In her sweatshirt and shorts, she was no longer warm; the night air felt like menthol on her bare legs. She watched as the other university students swarmed Main Street, crowding into the oversized wooden booths at the Cornerstone, streaming in and out of the sneaker store, lining up to get into the bar — the R&R — holding their fake IDs

aloft. She knew she shouldn't feel self-conscious — no
one could guess what she was up to — and yet she
felt as guiltily conspicuous as a black-masked thief in
a jewelry store after dark. She flushed every time
someone she knew passed by and tossed her a casual
wave or "hi." She smiled back stiffly, trying to tele-
graph to them not to linger, angry at them for not
being Sue.

Leigh began to pace; it was no help in conjuring
Sue, but it burned off a little of the gathering
anxiety at the small of her back. She sneaked a
furtive glance down the street that curved off Main
and led to the more obscure part of town, where the
Sun Motel was located and where she and Sue had a
reservation for the night. It had taken no small
amount of planning and scheming; they had both had
to lie to Mel. That alone disoriented Leigh; it had
always been Sue whom she and Mel had worked to
keep in the dark. They should have had so much in
common, all three of them, so much to share and say
to each other. Instead, it struck Leigh more and
more, mostly what they had were secrets.

Leigh continued to scan. The crowd was starting
to thin now, as everyone settled down to meals or
parties. She squinted hard down Main Street, her
mouth dry, jittery at the glimpse of every long-limbed
brunette who might, in coming closer, transform
herself into Sue. Leigh glanced at her watch. It was
7:07, April fifth, a month and a half till graduation.
She was on the threshold of some new life, one
fantasized about but still unimaginable, a life that
would shed forever summers off, and autumns whose
very scent meant the beginning of another whole year

spent gorging herself on books and reading and ideas. She did not even know yet how much she would miss it, but she felt mournful already, and forced herself to concentrate, to memorize Main Street and its colorful storefronts, and the tall, stone arch across the street that marked the entrance to campus.

"Leigh! Leigh, what are you doing here?" a voice called, jolting her back to the moment. It was Mel, somehow before her, her strong, square-jawed face and surprised gray eyes just an arm's length away. The ground tilted for a second and there was a pressure in her chest, like a finger at her breastbone, tapping. Her face burned, all the way to her earlobes. She had told Mel she was going to a study group tonight, clear on the other side of campus.

Mel was standing there, her eyebrows leveling to match her lips, which were pressed thin and straight. Leigh realized slowly that Mel was waiting, and that she would have to answer.

They had met at the beginning of the year, in Spanish class. Leigh had noticed Mel because her grammar was terrible but her accent the real, rolling thing. Mel had no explanation. She was born and raised in Kansas, on a farm her family owned and that she planned to run one day, not more than a hundred miles from campus. She supposed it was just instinct.

They had needed to wait until one or the other's roommate was away; it was one of the awkward things about being gay in a dorm. You could pay off your roommate to leave for the night if you wanted to smuggle in a man. Any kind of man: the spindly, pock-marked runners or the stiff-collared engineering majors or the glazed, inarticulate druggies. But if it was another woman you wanted to bed, you had to wait for your roommate to leave of her own accord. You smiled sweetly and felt contempt for her as she left because she had no clue that her roomie was a lesbian, and you felt contempt for yourself because you wouldn't dare tell her.

So before they could sleep together that first time, they had had to wait two months. They had dinner first at the Cornerstone, to be sure the roommate was really gone. Leigh was so full of wanting Mel that by the time they got back to her room, she was tender to the touch. Mel's skin was like Ivory soap, she was like milk, the stark white plane of her stretched out in front of Leigh, offering up the shock of her brick-red nipples and auburn coiled hair, moist where Leigh parted her. Their sex was serious, ferocious, disorderly, exhausting. Neither of them was new to it, and yet together they made something different, something raw, unleashed, unpracticed and yet exactly right.

It was two A.M. before they stopped. Mel went over to the window and threw back the curtains. Moonlight poured in. "Makes me want to howl," Mel turned to say.

"You've been howling for hours, in case you haven't noticed," Leigh said. "In which case, you'd be the only one for miles who hasn't. I'm sure your neighbors will be glad to fill your roommate in when she comes back about what went on while she was away."

Mel padded barefoot back to the narrow dorm
bed. Leigh eyed her body frankly and admiringly. She
loved Mel's large, ripe, swaying breasts.

"I'm in trouble," Mel said.

"Oh, your roommate will get over it. Tell her you
picked up a linebacker at the R&R."

"No, not that." Mel's face was like a fist opening.
That's when she told Leigh about Sue. How they'd
been together almost four years. How Sue had been a
senior and Mel a freshman when they got together,
and how Sue owned a house that Mel lived in during
summers, and which she'd own half of once she
graduated and began paying her share of the mortgage. Sue was straight when Mel met her, she was
engaged, but she'd left the guy. She'd never been
with another woman besides Mel, and Mel loved her.

The news was like a series of small body blows.
Leigh shivered, but she was too stunned to think to
pull the sheets around her. Leigh told herself she was
not in love with Mel, had no plans to be, but she
was proud. "So what am I doing here?"

"You just" — Mel couldn't look at her — "just
happened to me."

"You've known for months we were going to end
up in bed. This *didn't* just happen," Leigh said.

"I didn't think it really would."

"Why?"

"Because then I knew I'd have to leave Sue, and
that was hard to get used to."

The moon slipped behind a film of clouds; darkness pressed in from all sides. Leigh liked to win, she
admitted it. But she wasn't ready for a house, a
mortgage, monogamy. She was going home to New
York City when she graduated. She was going to be a

book editor and become famous. Those were her
plans. She knew danger and heartbreak were part of
her destiny.

They were still damp from their first sex, and
already the rhythm of every fight they would ever
have was clear to Leigh. She put her hand on Mel's
cheek, dragged her hand up into her hair, felt the
heat of her scalp. "You can't leave Sue," she said.
"I'd like to meet her."

That was how she stalled. But the rest was Mel's
idea. Leigh refused to take any responsibility for it.

The table rocked, first one way, then the other.
The three of them shifted shyly, each trying to right
it by withdrawing, then leaning back in. On the
jukebox, flashing red and yellow in the corner like a
roadside wreck, decade-old disco played. Women in
plaid shirts with barber-cut hair, women like Leigh
had never seen before, shuffled on the dance floor.
Pool balls cracked like an approaching storm. Mel
ordered another round.

"I know this place from home," Mel explained,
apologized. "I came out in this bar. Kissed my first
girl. But it's not New York, Leigh."

"I don't care at all," Leigh said. And she didn't.
Sue's Camaro was parked outside. They had driven
over from campus, joking loudly, but now all Leigh's
bravery was gone. Sue was elegant. Her neck was
long and graceful. Her fingers were thin, her wrists
fine-boned and fluid. Her eyebrows were thick and
arched, and when she looked at Leigh, it was with

such sympathy and good humor that Leigh felt completely uncovered.

It was a terrible thing. Because six months had gone by and now she was in love with Mel, against her plan. Mel who was without irony and cynicism of any kind, who was as quick to laughter and slow to grudges as a child, who made the kind of sounds in bed that Leigh ran through her head in class as though it was the very sound track of sex. Loving Mel had threaded itself into the air. It was as certain as her own breathing, and yet she didn't dare say it, didn't dare admit it to Mel. To Mel, it would mean something had to be done, but Leigh just wanted to feel it.

Mel got up and led Sue to the dance floor. Leigh watched from her wobbly chair. Jealousy washed up from her gut, made the back of her throat bitter. She was jealous of Sue, jealous of Mel. She was sodden with it.

Then she reminded herself she didn't have to be. Mel had been going home on weekends, telling Sue how it might be, what they might try. Sue resisted, was wounded and suspicious, but then was gradually reassured and intrigued. There would have to be rules, Sue warned, but what those rules were she did not make clear. Meanwhile, during the week, at school, Leigh had Mel, Mel was hers alone. They memorized their roommates' class schedules, and when either room was free, they bolted the door and stepped out of their clothes on the way to bed. They'd leave an hour later, not washing their hands, keeping the other's scent close for as long as they could. Sometimes unexpectedly one of the roommates

wouldn't come home, usually Mel's, and she'd call
Leigh at one A.M. Leigh would dress and go over, and
undress.

Her sleep suffered, or rather, the regular patterns
of it. She did not envy any language its twenty words
for snow, but she did think she could make use of
twenty words for sleep. There was the deep, blotted-
out sleep of exhaustion, the broken, restless sleep of
anxious dreams that rubbed like sand under her
eyelids, the bracing nap she taught herself to take in
between classes. Her whole life felt reduced to those
three states: the trance of study, of sleep, of sex.

Mel and Sue were moving well together, although
Mel was a better dancer. She was natural, spon-
taneous. Sue was more careful, premeditated, but she
was so finely etched, so long-torsoed and well-made,
that she drew all the eyes in the room, anyway.

Mel gestured for Leigh to join them. That was
their plan, how they had rehearsed it as she and Mel
lay head to hip in their tiny dorm bed. Sue would be
made to think it was the first time for them all.
That would be the lie.

Leigh danced with them. She didn't know whose
rhythm to match, so she matched no one's. Sue
reached out and took Leigh's hand, laced her fingers
through, one by one, slowly, turned Leigh to face her
fully, smiled. Mel drew close, put her arms around
both her lovers' waists, gave Leigh a look of such
frank hunger that Leigh lowered her eyes and hoped
Sue didn't see.

They drove back toward campus, Sue at the
wheel, Mel in the passenger seat, Leigh in the back.

Night swirled outside the car, but inside, it seemed
lit with their commingled fear and ardor. Sue stopped
the car outside the Sun Motel. Mel jumped out, her
wallet already palmed, and headed inside for the
front desk.

Sue turned and leaned her back against the driver
door, took Leigh in with a languid gaze. "This is
pretty crazy, huh? Not something we respectable
types are supposed to do."

"Respectable, well, I don't know . . ." Leigh said,
laughing, looking away. Their near whispers in the
dark hollow of the car seemed suddenly more intimate than a kiss.

"I wouldn't even be thinking about this, you
know, if I didn't think you were someone special,"
Sue said. "There's something sweet about you, I can
tell. You don't like that to show, but it does." She
smiled.

"Well, I . . ." Leigh had forgotten how to speak.
She looked helplessly at Sue, with her eyes as glossy
as onyx, the dimple pressed into her chin.

"I don't want you to think I don't love Mel," Sue
said.

I do, too, Leigh thought to say. Instead, she said,
"I know you do. She loves you, too."

The passenger door flew open, and Mel was there,
springing up and down on her toes. "Come on, now,
no time to waste," she said, dangling a key from two
fingers.

The room was simple, almost seminarian in its
sparseness. Two double beds, covered in clay-colored
bedspreads, were separated by a wooden night table.

There was a desk against one wall. The rug was thin. Mel shut the door without turning on a light, went over and threw back the curtains. It was a welcome and familiar gesture, and Leigh was grateful for it. It gave her some measure of courage.

Leigh saw that she had to be the one to start. Mel was overeager, she would give them away. Sue had almost disappeared into a column of darkness between the beds. Leigh went over and stood before her, brave and anonymous now in shadow, and began to unbutton her own blouse. Mel stepped behind Sue, and tugged Sue's sweater free from her jeans, up over her head. Sue allowed it, and allowed Leigh to kiss her then, and to cup her breast under her sheer, shiny bra, trace her thumb over the smear of nipple. Leigh felt a pulse of desire begin between her legs. If there was any caution in the air among them, any whisper of doubt or compunction, it was stilled.

After that, it was easy to lose track, important even. Years later, Leigh was able to retrieve only random images, the chronology and details having been lost to the swamp of impression, gilded by lust. Leigh remembered the wincing sound Sue made when Leigh had her mouth on her. She remembered having to squeeze her eyes shut tight, the way she would on a fast ride, while Mel went down on her at the same time that Sue was kissing her, and being dizzied by the lapping of tongues. She remembered her own fingertips, pruned from so much wetness. She remembered submitting, and devouring, and coming and coming and coming.

Eventually, sleep overtook them. Leigh moved to the other bed for more comfort during the sprawl of slumber. She lay on her back and watched as Sue and Mel breathed into each other's faces as they slept, their arms and legs jumbled together like dolls' in a toy box. She did not feel exiled; she felt completely a part. The web of their sex stretched across the distance, filled the room, would encompass them no matter how far one or the other moved away.

It was the first and last night she would feel that way, although they all slept together many more nights. Each time, a new shard of self-consciousness and self-interest wedged itself somewhere among them. Leigh began to worry that she or Mel would reveal themselves, that their prior intimacy would be detected in some small, skilled maneuver or smile of recognition. She began to understand that if Mel lingered too long over her, a tight coil of panic would rise in Sue. During the week, she and Mel continued to make love alone — although each swore to Sue it hadn't, didn't, wouldn't happen. But now Mel seemed angry, competitive. She seemed to want Leigh to come harder, come more, than she did with Sue. For her part, Leigh felt weighed down by her love for Mel, pressed to the ground and flattened by it, even while she felt buoyant, light-footed at the sight of Sue, at the thought of Sue. Outside of bed, the same dramas played out, only without the ache of lust. There was no relief.

This night they had driven to Sue's house, as had recently become their habit. Too many nights at the Sun Motel had grown embarrassing and expensive. Though they never spoke of it, going to Sue's house had meant crossing some line, and they had all been reluctant to do it. Because this was soon to be Sue and Mel's house, the beginning of their official life together as a couple. The house, nestled in its shrubbed suburbia, made them briefly shy together again, at first. But now, they were brazen even here.

Tonight they started on the couch, undressing each other in stages, moving to the bed only after they'd made a pile of their clothes, the slicked panties and coiled bras. Mel had moved a Tiffany lamp into the room, making a weird glow of purple and rose wash over them. Mel had put herself in charge of arranging games. Sue pressed Leigh to the bed on her back, kissing her for long stretches, and Mel crouched at the far end, tasting each of them in turn. Leigh had no body; she had no sight or thought. All of her that remained was sensation and swell and scent.

At the house, Leigh had her own room, down the hall. She had been fully submerged, dumb with slumber, when she was jangled awake. "Shhhh," came the sound. "Move over." It was Sue.

"What is it?" Leigh asked.

"I missed you." Sue began to kiss her again; Leigh felt bruised with kisses. "I had a dream about you," Sue said.

"What about me?" Leigh felt a drumbeat of desire and dread. She wanted Sue to choose her, didn't she? But she wanted Mel to, also. She worried that Mel would wake, come in, find them.

"That you asked me to marry you." Sue bit her bottom lip, smiled coyly.

"What did you say?" Leigh whispered. She fought

herself and lost. She traced circles up Sue's thigh, slipped two fingers inside her.

"I woke up. Then I came here." Sue hid her face against Leigh's shoulder, began to grind against her fingers. "We can't . . . do this here," she breathed. "I want to be with you alone, just once. I want to know what it feels like."

And then what, and then what? a voice in Leigh's head demanded. But she ignored it. The plan was made: they would meet, seven P.M. the next night, on the corner, then to the Sun Motel. A new set of lies. Leigh had lost track of the truth.

Mel and Leigh took a booth in the Cornerstone Cafe. "You've slept with her alone, haven't you?" Mel asked.

"No," Leigh said. She was gratified that this small sliver was true.

"But you were going to, weren't you?" Mel said. "Isn't that what tonight is about? The fact that you and Sue both coincidentally had plans so I couldn't reach either of you?"

Leigh said nothing. If Mel had found them out so easily, it must have shown, it must have all shown, how each of them, privately, was hoping to be chosen. Leigh saw the tears standing in Mel's eyes. She took in all the details of Mel's face, the way she moved, shifted in the booth, laced her fingers together on the table, and knew she loved her. But it easn't enough to stop her from wondering where Sue was. Had Sue spotted Mel on Main Street and stayed

away? Or was she merely late? Was she outside on
the corner now, pacing? Was she at the Sun Motel,
awkwardly asking if Leigh was registered? Would she
think Leigh had stood her up? Leigh didn't want to
lie to Mel. It would get them nowhere. Just deeper
into the labyrinth. And it would change everything
about them together.

"Fine. Just stonewall," Mel said.

"I — I don't know what —"

"I'll leave her right now," Mel said, reaching
across the table and gripping Leigh's wrist. "Just
don't meet her. I'll tell her it's over. I'll come to
New York with you. Let me come to New York with
you."

One of them, Leigh saw all at once, had to lose
everything. They had briefly stumbled into some time
warp, but it would end, and soon. And then the
ordered way of the world would descend over them
like a net, and only two of them could be caught.
Sacrifices were waiting to be made. She had known it
all along, of course, but she had not faced it.

Her teacup, the table, Mel's face, everything
blurred. Leigh trapped one tear with her middle
finger, ground it into her cheekbone, silently
commanded the others to dry up. She thought of Sue
alone, in her house, Mel gone, abandonment the
reward for her cooperation in their selfish scheme.
And as much as Leigh loved Mel now, this moment,
she knew that love wouldn't survive the move. Mel
could not simply be repotted in New York. They
would grow distant, maybe even hostile, when their
real differences were revealed. They might not be
able to salvage any part of their affection.

"No," Leigh said. "You can't come to New York."

"Of course I can. I'm doing it." Mel began looking frantically around for the waitress, as if she meant to bolt and catch a plane this second.

"No. I don't want you to," Leigh said.

"Don't worry," Mel said. "It won't be easy telling Sue but I —"

"I don't love you. I never said I did," Leigh said. She pulled in her breath hard.

Mel was still frowning into the distance for the waitress, and now she didn't turn her head at all. Instead she just lowered her eyes, studied the far corner of the buffed wooden table between them.

Leigh could see that Mel didn't believe her, not really, not down in the pores of her where she knew Leigh best. But still, it was too searing an insult; it was too risky to debate.

"Don't meet her, then. Don't even talk to her again. Can you do that last thing for me?" Mel asked, speakaing slowly and quietly. Leigh could meet her eyes only briefly, then she looked away. She managed to nod.

"I've loved *you*, though," Mel said. "I have." She stood.

She had seconds, Leigh realized, to change the way it would all turn out. Would Mel even tell Sue she had seen her tonight — or would she let Sue think she had been stood up? Would Sue guess what had really transpired, anyway — tonight and the rest of their nights?

When she looked up, Mel was gone. There were just the hanging plants and the shiny wooden tables, and the crowd of people, not a single one of whom meant a thing to her. Maybe, Leigh thought, she was as rotten as she appeared to Mel just now; maybe she hadn't loved either one of them, or at least not well enough. Maybe none of it mattered, really, at all. And that was the last lie, then, the one she told herself, the one that made it possible to live with, the one she might one day believe.

Tattoo

Elisabeth Nonas

Eve had tattoos. Some you could see, like the mice that chased each other around her left wrist. That blue-black tattoo color. A yin-yang symbol on her inner forearm. On her biceps a runic-looking symbol of her sign — Scorpio. All I could think was how much it must have hurt her to get them.

Eve had only recently started working at the West Hollywood shop where I used to go sometimes to buy expensive presents for Laurel. Even after thirteen

years I had still liked to surprise my lover with a
little treat once in a while, for no special occasion. It
was easy to be a romantic, safely cushioned as I was
by the years behind us and the years I assumed
stretched ahead. My assumptions and trust had been
blasted apart, however, when Laurel left me suddenly.
Well, suddenly to me, and I did whatever I could to
keep myself going.

I had stopped in at the store to find something
that might cheer me up, but looking around had
made me sadder. I was on my way out the door
when something colorful caught my eye. Eve was
wearing one of the silk jackets off the display. A
kimonolike affair, cerise with yellow trim. She was
reaching above her head to hang an angel from a
hook on the wall. The sleeves of the jacket slipped
down her milky arms, and I saw her tattoos for the
first time.

I gave her a hand with the angel, almost dropping
it because I was so distracted by the tattoos. "I have
more," she said. "Here," she pointed behind her back
with her thumb, as if I could see under her clothes,
"and here." She yanked the sleeve up above her
elbow. The tail of a dragon disappeared around her
arm.

Didn't they hurt? I hated to ask the question and
risk sounding too vanilla. I tried to think beyond the
pain, but I couldn't imagine why people got tattoos,
why they'd do that to their bodies — not just the
pain, but the permanence.

Impossible not to touch. I realized only after a
minute or so that I had her arm in my hands and
was twisting it to take it all in. "Sorry," I muttered,
letting go.

"No problem. People like to look."

I didn't want to be people. I wanted to be more contained or reserved or something. More like myself. Trouble was, I no longer knew who that was.

We talked a bit longer.

I took to dropping in on my way home from the office. I didn't buy anything. I just talked to Eve. Even after I moved out of my house and into temporary quarters in Silver Lake, I stopped by. I'd come to depend on my little chats with Eve. They smoothed out the end of the day.

I hadn't been on a date in over thirteen years. Or noticed, really noticed, women. I saw Eve, though, even through the drapey, loose clothing she wore. After that first day I didn't touch her, but I couldn't stop thinking about her soft skin.

I learned a little more about her. She made angels. She'd made the one she'd been hanging when I met her. She used her dining room as her studio and had thousands of ceramic angels waiting to be decorated. The whole angel trend was a little cute for my taste, but her angels were sort of sweet. She made them with very real, pink cheeks, and gave them blue or green eyes that followed you. "The angels are just a job. I paint the Blessed Mother also. That's my art. It's not that I see visions, but I do feel protected by her."

"By the Blessed Mother?" Just a simple question; I tried to keep all judgment out of my voice.

Eve nodded. "And sometimes by Jesus as well."

I didn't think this was going to work. Talk of Jesus always scared me, especially in a prospective bed partner, and it did appear that that's where Eve and I were headed.

We'd done all this talking. It seemed only natural to invite her out. *Natural for whom,* I thought after I'd done it and she'd accepted.

At dinner Eve wore a black sleeveless blouse that showed off her tattoos. I took her hand across the table. This was the first time I'd touched her since that day five weeks earlier when I had helped arrange her angel. I brought her hand to my lips, kissed the inside of her wrist, touched three or four of the mice with my tongue. I looked at her face over our hands, tried to invite her to bed just using my eyes.

My finger outlined the yin and the yang of that ancient symbol tattooed on the smooth white skin of her inner forearm. I moved my hand up a little to embrace her elbow. The dragon on her shoulder was red and yellow, green and blue. Its eyes blazed. My thumb traced the flames shooting from its mouth. "Didn't these hurt?"

She shrugged. "You only go for small bits, never more than three hours at a time." She sketched a circle on the back of my hand. "You ever think of getting one?"

I shook my head.

"You ought to. Though it's hard to stop at one."

"How much does it hurt?"

Eve reached over and pinched the skin inside my forearm. "About like that."

The pain was minimal but persistent. After a few seconds I wanted to brush her hand away, annoyed, as if to swat at a mosquito. Then a kind of exquisite sting set in and I hoped her nails would leave a mark.

Eve released my skin. "What do you think?"

"Would you like to come home with me?" To hide my embarrassment I rattled on about how we'd already covered the safer sex discussion — she'd been celibate for years, and I'd been entrenched in a monogamous relationship.

I felt Eve's bare foot on top of my shoe. I stopped talking, took a very deliberate bite of food, making sure to chew even though my salad was rendered a tasteless paste by the charge that bolted up my leg right to my clit. I swallowed as Eve's foot walked up my leg, down, and came to rest again on top of my shoe.

We split the check, then I drove us to my place. We'd come in my car; hers overflowed with angels.

I trembled when Eve first kissed me. We stood just inside the door to my apartment. My first kiss since I'd been left. I'd wanted Eve from the moment we'd met. Now here we were, and I wasn't sure I'd remember what to do. She helped. She leaned forward and kissed me softly, openmouthed. I put my hands on her shoulders and leaned toward her, matching her weight with my own, her light touch with my own. I was a little shaky, and when I brushed my hand across the top of her breast I

surprised myself because I felt soft skin — somehow
I'd managed to unbutton her blouse and didn't know
how or when I had.

My body possessed more memory than my brain.
Fingers instinctively undid buttons, tongue grazed
neck, ears. My hips rotated before I could even send
them the message, before I knew I wanted to be
moving against this other body. My knees buckled a
little; I let out a soft groan.

Eve suggested we move somewhere more comfortable. "How about over there?" She nodded in the
direction of the living room couch.

I took her hand and led her to my bedroom.

I hadn't prepared the place for seduction. I'd only
been living in the apartment for a month. I hadn't
bought groceries, much less romantic supplies. I was
afraid Eve would catch on to how out of practice I
was. Not a candle in the house, not a radio, nothing
for atmosphere. Still, the air in the room seemed
thick — underwater almost — as I moved with Eve to
the bed. My breath came in shallow spurts, my heart
pounded heavily. I turned when I got to the
nightstand. At least my halogen lamp had two
settings; I switched it to the dimmer one and set
about remembering how to make love to a woman
who wasn't my mate.

I was unprepared for Eve's back.

Angel wings sprouted from her spine, swept down
to the curve of her ass. They appeared three-
dimensional, graceful, and oddly practical, as if flight
were a real possibility. They stood out because they
hovered over a body of water, a sea or lake, waves in
the Japanese tradition that would dwarf any ship

that challenged them. The effect was like looking
down on that body of water from a great height.

I traced my fingers over a thin black outline
bordering white foam. Brilliant blues: cerulean,
sapphire and turquoise. Brilliant and surreal, so
bright against Eve's smooth white skin.

I wondered how deep it went, how far down did
the colors go? The blues had depth. I was surprised
my fingers didn't submerge, sink into the water, feel
the pull of the tide that dragged the wave up from
the shore of her spine.

"What made you do this?" I whispered, awestruck.

I touched each feathered wing. Tears came to my
eyes and I dipped down to the water again. My
fingers skimmed the surface, danced over the current.

Eve answered me, something about commemora-
ting events in her life, wanting them made visible.

I didn't need to hear her words. I could feel the
answer in the sweep of the wing, the motion of the
waves.

I thought about scratching a reminder somewhere
on my own body. Laurel's and my dates — when she
walked into my life, when she left it. Maybe on my
arm where I could see them, on my palm so I would
never forget. Or maybe a bleeding heart on my
breast.

I had been marked by Laurel's leaving, marked by
my years with her. Their imprint was deep under my
skin — how deep I wasn't sure, couldn't be sure —
indelible as any tattoo and as colorful as the real

ones before me. The blacks and purples of the first month of her leaving, that first month when I didn't know if I would make it. The black/blue wash like the veins in my wrists that sang to me. The awful browns of that dark time, shot through with red, blood maybe, violence. Those colors hid the designs of our years together, the outlines of our house, the dogs, the trees we'd planted. Etched in pain and permanent now, but not visible the way Eve's were. One would need to know where to look, how to hold my body to the light, to see them.

All the milestones were inside me, tangible. Tactile and present. I didn't need a tattoo to remind me.

"Oooh, that feels so good." Eve had started to move under my hand.

I'd almost forgotten her there as I traced my invisible tattoos, scars of my years with Laurel, her marks on me, a brand.

"Don't stop," Eve said.

I climbed on top of her, straddled her back, moved against her ass. Still tracing the waves, the soaring wings.

"Yes," she said.

Eyes open I bent over Eve, descended from a great height, dizzy with fear and loss. I dipped under the wings and touched my tongue to her back, to the bright blue waters. I tasted salt. I opened my mouth wider and drank.

valentine@intouch.com

Karin Kallmaker

```
Roxanne has entered the Family Room.
Gozer (to Roxanne), `Hi, long time no see."
Roxanne waves to Gozer. "I have a friend with
     me. She wanted to see what the net was
     like."
```

C.J. looked over her shoulder at Lisa. "You don't have to type all that stuff, there's shortcuts. Watch." Slowly, so Lisa could see what she was doing, C.J. typed `.smiles` `My friend's name is Lisa,` then pressed the enter key. Her screen displayed:

> Roxanne smiles and says, `My friend's name is
> Lisa."

"Cool," Lisa said.

"That's one of the reasons I like moo's better than chat. You can really develop a personality beyond what you say."

"Why did you pick Roxanne for a nickname?"

"After the Sting song," C.J. said. "Or from *Cyrano de Bergerac*. Take your pick."

> Gozer says, `Hi Lisa."
> Deckor8r says, `Hi Lisa."

The screen filled with a series of hellos to Lisa. C.J. grimaced as the name "God'sGift" appeared. "Watch out for that guy," she said to Lisa. "He's got one thing on his mind and doesn't believe I'm not interested."

> God'sGift winks at you. `And what are the
> luscious Roxanne and her friend Lisa up to
> this late at night? Something I'd want to
> watch, maybe?"
> Roxanne regards God'sGift coolly, then turns
> to speak to Gozer. `Lisa is curious about
> the net." She glances at God'sGift and rolls
> her eyes. `And nothing else. I told her
> this was the best MOO."
> God'sGift says, `I'm sure you can change her
> mind. I thought all you LADIES were out to
> convert the innocent." =)

C.J. grunted. "He says he's joking, but he's not."

"Joking?"

"The equal sign and parenthesis. If you tip your

head to the left they make a smiley face. That's
shorthand for joking or laughing."
"Oh." Lisa sounded puzzled. C.J.'s fingers flew
over the keyboard.

> Roxanne (to Gozer) "Show Lisa you being
> unhappy."
> Gozer :(

Lisa chuckled. "I get it. You could get quite
creative."
"You can also look at people to see how they
describe themselves. Like this."

> Roxanne looks at Gozer. GOZER: School is
> killing me so don't tell me I should be
> studying. I am recruiting minions for the
> mighty and powerful Order of Gozer when all
> non-Gozers shall be consumed by an evil
> torg. Gozer is strong and powerful. Those
> who say Gozer is 90-pound weakling will be
> consumed first.

"I think Gozer's is one of the more honest
descriptions," C.J. said, smiling. "God'sGift says he
looks like Fabio, only better."
"Eeewwwww," Lisa said. "Yes, well, an inflated
consciousness is hypnotized by itself."

> God'sGift would like to take Roxanne and Lisa
> to his private room.

"A weather balloon would feel like a pea next to
this guy's ego," C.J. said. "I'm going to gag him.
That way I won't see anything he types." Her fingers
flew over the keyboard.

```
Roxanne is now gagging God'sGift.
Roxanne whispers 'What a jerk" to Gozer.
```

"When I whisper to others, no one can read it but me and them," she said to Lisa. "It can get real confusing because you can have private and public conversations going at once. If you forget to whisper it can get embarrassing."

```
        Lil_Bunny_Foo_Foo has entered the room.
        Deckor8r morphs into FieldMouse.
        FieldMouse runs screaming from the room.
```

Lisa laughed. "Some people are incredibly quick on the keyboard!" She sipped from her diet Coke. "Well, thanks for showing me how the moo-thing works. It is more lively than chat rooms at America Online. It could be stimulating if the people were more interesting." She patted C.J.'s shoulder.

"This is pretty lame," C.J. said. "But I like moo's because it feels like a real place instead of a window on the screen. We could teleport over to the hot tub, or see if there's a group in the poetry room. Though the last time I was there they were talking about deconstruction of post-modern metaphors."

"And me a plain ol' ordinary closet Emily Dickinson case," Lisa said. "How do you find out about a moo?"

"Well, I found this one because my Internet service had it in their directory. Or you can ask around the newsgroups on Usenet. Moo's can be unreliable because they run on someone's mainframe and you actually sign on to the mainframe with your persona and password. So if the mainframe's down, your moo is down, too. Or gone forever. If I meet

someone I like on a moo I get their e-mail address
because you never know if you'll run into them
again."

Lisa sighed and looked at her watch. "I suppose
we should get back to work."

"You're right," C.J. said. "Let me sign off. I don't
want to use up my work online allotment moo-ing
around."

> Roxanne waves to everyone. 'We have to go back
>   to work. Good night all!"
> Gozer says, 'Work? At this hour."
> Roxanne (to Gozer) It's not that late on the
>   West Coast. Only 11. We're working on a
>   presentation rush-rush.
> Gozer . o O (I'll bet it's marketing or adver-
>   tising . . .)

"What do the dot and zeros mean?" Lisa pointed
to the symbols after Gozer's name.

"Oh, those are thought bubbles."

"That's clever," Lisa said. "I thought it would be
hard to express emotions at the keyboard."

> Roxanne . o O (Advertising is a perfectly
>   respectable career for a Comp Lit computer
>   geek!)

Lisa laughed into C.J.'s ear. "What else could we
do with a Liberal Arts education?"

> Roxanne (to Gozer) Gotta go, dude. Talk to you
>   tomorrow night maybe. Bye!
> Gozer waves to Roxanne.
> Roxanne has disconnected.

Lisa drained the last of her diet Coke, then

favored C.J. with a long, steady gaze. C.J. hadn't realized that Lisa's eyes were such a smoky gray. "Do you tell everyone on the net you're a lesbian?"

C.J. nodded. "It's in my description for all to see."

"But you said you can't take descriptions at face value."

"Depends," C.J. said. "A horse's ass is still easy to spot, description or not. On the net, the keyboard is the great equalizer. You don't know what anyone looks like, or where they went to school, or what they do for a living. You don't know if they're straight or gay or in-between. You can only judge them by what they type. That's probably the allure — anything can happen."

Lisa stared at a point somewhere behind C.J.'s left shoulder. "Except in real life. That always goes the same way. After Ron I've just been — I can't make the effort anymore. Men take so much of it and it's just not right for me anymore."

"I'm sorry," C.J. said. She didn't know what else to say. "Dating's a bitch, isn't it?"

"No easier from your perspective?" Lisa was still staring just over C.J.'s left shoulder.

"Not at all. She-Whose-Name-Shall-Never-Pass-My-Lips was a bitch, too."

Lisa's laugh turned into a sigh. "The hardest part is coming right out and telling someone you'd like to get to know them. Especially when they think you're not compatible. You know, they've already made up their minds about you." She met C.J.'s gaze for a nanosecond, then stood up and stretched. "Lord

knows I could do something more useful with my
evenings than work. Or watch American Gladiators,
Ron's idea of a cheap date."
   C.J. shuddered. "Sometimes life is better behind
the shelf."
   Lisa blinked at her, then smiled oddly. "How
apropos, as usual." Lisa headed toward her office.
"I'll send you the rest of the text in about fifteen
minutes."
   "Okey-dokey," C.J. called after her. Lisa was a
good co-worker and easily the best account exec to
work with. She was funny and interesting, even for a
straight woman. Lesbian-chauvinist, she chided
herself.

> Splash! Roxanne enters the hot tub.
> The Hot Tub: The water is perfect! Stay and
>   relax. Guest4, sAmMy, RogerCorman7, Neon
>   and Klondike are here.
> Guest4 takes a drink from the bar.
> sAmMy looks at you. ROXANNE: She walks in
>   averageness, like the interminable time be-
>   tween 4 and 5 when work seems like it will
>   never end. Of cloudy climes and starless
>   skies; And all that's worst of gray and
>   dull could be changed in an instant if
>   you're a Lesbian who likes Byron, too.
> Roxanne waves at everyone.

   C.J. fished her slippers out from under the desk
and wrapped her bathrobe more tightly around her.

Summer in San Francisco had set in with a vengeance.

> RogerCorman7 says, "I'm a director."
>
> sAmMy (to Roxanne) "I don't think we've met."
>
> Roxanne (to sAmMy) "I think you're right. How do you do?"
>
> Neon . o O (And I'm Jimmy Carter.)
>
> sAmMy (to Roxanne) 'What would you like to talk about? "
>
> Roxanne looks at sAmMy. SAMMY: One of these is true: I am 19, unbelievably rich and very good looking. Women go wild over my excellent sense of humor and my ability to be sensitive to their needs. I cried when I saw Beaches.
>
> Roxanne (to sAmMy) 'Let me guess. You're 19."
>
> sAmMy smiles. 'But age is a state of mind, isn't it?"
>
> Guest4 turns the hot tub lights on and off.
>
> Klondike (to RogerCorman7) 'What have you directed?"
>
> Splash! Howard_J._Nelson enters the hot tub.
>
> sAmMy (to Roxanne) It's crowded in here.

C.J. sighed and took a large swallow of her cooling tea. The crowd in the hot tub was as boring as the group in the living room.

> Howard_J._Nelson hands you his business card. "I specialize in getting financial aid for students."
>
> Guest4 (to Howard_J._Nelson) No selling on the net!
>
> Roxanne says, 'Let's boot him."
>
> sAmMy whispers to you, "I like a woman who takes charge."

A large sewer opens under Howard_J._Nelson.
He disappears from sight with a shriek of
dismay.
Klondike (to Roxanne) 'Quick thinking."
Roxanne looks at Klondike. KLONDIKE: Lick her,
she's creamy! Definitely Klondyke. Let's
play word games!

C.J. smiled. This was intriguing.

Roxanne (to Klondike) Thank you.
Klondike grins at Roxanne.
sAmMy (to Roxanne) 'Are you really a lesbian?"
Klondike looks at Roxanne with a quirked
eyebrow.
Roxanne (to sAmMy) 'Yes I am."
Klondike whispers "I know a quieter room" to
Roxanne.
sAmMy (to Roxanne) "I've always wondered what
lesbians do in bed."

"Give me a break," C.J. said. "Like I'm on the
net to satisfy your curiosity."

Roxanne (to sAmMy) 'Sleep, mostly."
Klondike laughs out loud and teleports out.
Roxanne joins Klondike.
The Garden of Earthly Delights: Birds chirp
softly in the background as you walk through
this warm, green garden. The ground is a
carpet of green grass which looks soft
enough to lie on. Klondike is here.

C.J. chewed her lip. No doubt she was supposed
to stretch out on the grass.

Klondike says, 'Do you like my room?"
Roxanne says, "It's lovely. But I was hoping

```
      to make a stop in the Poetry Room sometime
      tonight."
   Klondike runs her fingertips lightly over your
   lips. You tremble in response.
   Klondike says, "Are you sure?"
```

Ugh, C.J. thought. Pre-scripted sex telling me how
I feel. Just like real sex with What's-Her-Name twice
removed.

```
      Roxanne says, "I'm sure."
      Klondike teleports out.
```

How rude, C.J. thought. Can't take no for an
answer.

It was after midnight. C.J. told herself she really
ought to get some sleep. She reached for the dis-
connect button, then thought she would see if anyone
interesting — just for the sake of some adult conversation — was in the poetry room. The hot tubbers
tended to avoid poetry like the plague. She typed in
the jump command.

```
      Roxanne enters the Poetry Room.
      The Poetry Room: Chaises are scattered through-
      out this long, quiet room. Though the light
      is low from the French doors, wherever you
      sit there is enough light to read by.
      Bookshelves line the western wall. You can
      hear the tinkle of a fountain through the
      open French doors to the north. Keats5,
      Flaubert and Valentine are here.
   Keats5 says, "when man determined to destroy,
      himself he picked the was, of shall and
      finding only why, smashed it into because"
```

Oh, not him, C.J. thought.

Flaubert says, 'But cummings wasn't talking about religion, per se."

Keats5 exclaims, 'He didn't have to, because it was the discourse of his time!"

Valentine selects a book and exits north through the French doors.

Good thinking, Valentine, C.J. thought. She followed Valentine into the adjoining room.

The Conservatory: Wrought iron benches painted white are nestled at intervals along the greenhouse. To the south, there is an arbor of roses. Valentine is here.

Roxanne looks at Valentine. VALENTINE: As you glance at her, you find only unfinished edges. Now, today, I shall sing beautifully for my friends' pleasure. Valentine looks back at you.

Roxanne says, 'Hello, Valentine. Am I disturbing you?"

Valentine (to Roxanne) 'Not at all. I was hoping someone would come along who didn't want to talk about religion as the discourse of poets."

Valentine looks at Roxanne.

Good, C.J. thought. Now she knows I'm gay so we can just get that out of the way.

Roxanne sits down on a bench and sniffs delicately at a Calla Lilly. 'That quote in your description — it seems familiar."

Valentine smiles to herself. 'You'll get it sooner or later. I also like Byron, by the way."

There was a lull and C.J. tried to think of something to fill it in.

> Roxanne asks, 'Do you think there are any poets today?"
>
> Valentine nods. 'Yes! As long as there is the unsayable needing to be said."
>
> Valentine adds, 'But they hardly get patrons any more, so my private theory is that most of them are strumming a guitar along with the poems to make a living."
>
> Roxanne says, 'Well, that would explain Bob Dylan. It's not his singing voice that attracted the following. =) "
>
> Valentine says, 'His musical talent had something to do with it. ;) But some folk singers are writing some amazing poetry."
>
> Roxanne reels off, 'Tracy Chapman, Michelle Shocked, Suzanne Vega . . ."
>
> Valentine smiles and says, "I agree . . . the women acquit themselves very well!"

Encouraged, C.J. straightened up in her chair and abandoned all thoughts of disconnecting. So she likes Byron, C.J. thought. But is she a *lesbian* who likes Byron? She read Valentine's description again.

> Roxanne says, "I really can't recall the poet who wrote that line in your description."
>
> Valentine winks slowly at Roxanne.
>
> Valentine disconnects.

"Damn!" C.J. stared at her screen in disbelief. She finally meets another woman interested in poetry with lesbian overtones and she turns out to be a flirt!

* * * * *

C.J. yawned so loudly that she was sure one of her cubicle neighbors would comment. They remained fixated on their work and C.J. wiped her bleary eyes. From the time she'd disconnected, until nearly four a.m., she'd looked through every book of poetry by women she had. Valentine surely wouldn't have a man's verse in her description. She'd grabbed an hour or two of sleep, but only after she'd thumbed through all of her Adrienne Rich and about half of the Audre Lourde. Olga Broumas was still to come, and then Marge Piercy . . . the list was a long one. Nobody, outside of a university maybe, had read more lesbian poetry than she had. And she'd found nothing to lead her to the elusive Valentine.

A shadow fell over her screen and C.J. glanced over her shoulder. Lisa smiled in her usual cheerful way, though she looked a little tired, and handed over a stack of notes.

"This is the last of it, I think. Will you be able to do slides with color?"

C.J. glanced at her watch. "The lab owes me a favor, so I could get them by two." To her embarrassment she suddenly yawned.

Lisa rested one hand on C.J.'s shoulder. "Late night?"

C.J. nodded. "I was searching for something."

"Aren't we all?" Lisa arched her eyebrows.

For some reason C.J. felt herself flush. She could hardly tell Lisa about Valentine. "I just hate mysteries."

Lisa laughed merrily as she left, leaving C.J. with

a vague feeling of having missed a joke somewhere. She was too sleepy to be funny.

       `*Valentine is not connected.*`

"Damn it, damn it, damn it!" CJ exclaimed. She could hardly display her wit and cunning to Valentine if Valentine wasn't signed on. She drummed her fingers on the mousepad, then irritably snapped off the C.D. player.

    `Info Valentine`
    `*Valentine is handle for valentine@intouch.`
    `com. Last sign on: Today, 9:41 p.m.*`

"Well if that doesn't beat all. I missed her by ten minutes. Damn bus." She'd worked late to help Lisa with another marketing presentation deck and then her bus had been forever making the long way up Geary. She was racking up the overtime hours, but it was eating into the time she wanted to spend tracking down the elusive and intriguing Valentine.

She thrummed her fingers on the keyboard, then realized she had another alternative. She now had Valentine's e-mail address. She thought for a moment, then composed an e-mail.

    `We seem to be just missing each other in the`
    `Poetry Room. I've figured out that quote`
    `in your description: Sappho. I'll give you`
    `one of my own:`
    `The balsamic day's ending, flaxen with drones`
    `and bees . . .`
    `Senses, with a love kiss,`
    `The beauty of similar lips.`

```
If you'd like to discuss we can meet in the
Poetry Room again after 10 pm pacific time.
======Roxannne======
```

The ball was back in Valentine's court. C.J. would have to bide her time.

C.J. leaned into Lisa's tiny office and handed over the originals for her Kitchen Delight campaign. "The overheads will be done in about ten minutes."

"I'll get Stacey going on making the copies. Thanks," Lisa said with sincerity. "I owe you again. Nobody works as fast as you do."

"Mention that often and loudly in the hearing of those who determine my bonuses," C.J. said.

Lisa was thumbing through the stack of paper. "That logo turned out nice, didn't it?" Abruptly she yawned, covering her mouth with a hand C.J. suddenly noticed was quite . . . elegant. Tapered fingers, manicured nails not too long . . .

A yawn seized C.J., too, and when she was finished she wiped tears out of her eyes and giggled. "That was your fault. You got me started."

"I was up too late," Lisa said. "I hate mysteries —"

Lisa's phone beeped and C.J. waved good-bye as Lisa answered it.

C.J.'s e-mail box stayed disappointingly empty and Valentine hadn't been online for several days. She

cruised over to a World Wide Web site and
downloaded some GIFs for her clip art collection,
then jumped to Usenet to read her favorite newsgroups.

She finished reading the new postings on
rec.arts.poetry.romantic and decided to check out
rec.arts.poetry.lesbians. There were several posts, and
she read the first two threads, posting a response to
one where the writer was asking if anyone knew of a
dissertation on lesbian content in the works of
Colette.

The next thread was titled "Help with a quote."
The original writer wanted help finding the entire
passage of a quote from an Audre Lourde essay. The
second writer offered help to the first, then asked for
similar help with Gertrude Stein. The third writer
didn't offer help, but followed up the thread with a
request of her own. As C.J. read it, she smiled to
herself.

> I've been up nights searching for the source
> of this quote. From the cadence, I'd guess
> it was 1880 to 1920? I do know it's by a
> lesbian. But the lesbians I can cross-
> reference in that time period are either
> not poets or didn't write such emotionally-
> edged stuff. There must be someone else.
> I'm new to studying lesbian poetry because
> I'm new to considering myself a lesbian.
> Please help me! Here's the quote:

And there it was, the quote she'd sent to
Valentine by e-mail. Well, well, well, thought C.J.
Valentine was just coming out. Her description had
said she had unfinished edges.

"Perhaps I can help her finish them," C.J. murmured to herself. Feeling more than a little smug, C.J. posted a follow-up for Valentine to read.

> That's cheating, Valentine. If you meet me after 10 tomorrow night, perhaps you'll be able to coax a hint out of me.

"Criminees, it's almost ten," C.J. squawked.

Lisa looked up from her proofreading with a gasp. "It can't be!"

"It is. I'm sorry, I've just got to run. I'm meeting someone." C.J. scrabbled up her notebook and switched off her computer.

"This can wait until tomorrow," Lisa said. "You are a prince for working late yet again. I can't leave you to the tender mercies of Muni — let me give you a lift home. I'll be back in a flash."

She returned in a few moments, a leather jacket over her brilliant turquoise silk blouse. The top button had come undone and C.J. thought, for just a moment, that Ron was a fool.

They were in Lisa's little Fiat — parks anywhere, Lisa said — when C.J. realized she was being bad company. She tried to stop worrying about missing Valentine online, but was only partly successful.

"Hot date?" Lisa looked over at her when the stopped for a light.

"Sort of. An appointment online."

"Someone interesting?"

"That's putting it mildly — turn left here. I'm at

the top of the hill. Thanks for the lift, I appreciate it."

"Don't mention it. Here?" Lisa double-parked while C.J. scrambled out of the low seat. "Flick your apartment light so I'll know you're in safe."

"I'll be fine, you don't have to wait," C.J. assured her.

"Company rules, ma'am. All riders seen safely home." Lisa smiled up at her and C.J. lost track of time for just a moment as the turquoise silk pulled tight across Lisa's cleavage. The streetlight illuminated Lisa's eyes and mouth and C.J. had to blink to make herself look away. Lisa was quite attractive, she realized. Except for being a straight woman, C.J. told herself quickly. It's been too long since you had a date, girl.

"I thought you were in a hurry," Lisa said.

"Ohmigosh," C.J. said, and she slammed the car door and dashed inside. Safe in her flat, which occupied half the upper floor of the house, she flickered her lights, and heard the drone of the Fiat continuing up the hill.

She threw herself in front of her computer. It was 10:02. By 10:04 she was online and Valentine wasn't. Valentine hadn't been on yet that night. Relieved, C.J. took a minute to get out of her work clothes, then checked for Valentine. Still not online. She dashed into the kitchen for a snack, then made some toast. By 10:15 she was beginning to think Valentine wasn't going to show. With a sigh, she asked for Valentine again and her heart leapt.

> *Valentine is in the Poetry Room Conservatory.*
> Roxanne joins Valentine.

Valentine says, "Sorry I'm late. I had to
    work."
Roxanne wonders if Valentine would like a hint.
Valentine . o O (Will she make me beg?)
Roxanne laughs. "I'll just tell you. Reneé
    Vivien, an American who wrote in French."
Valentine furiously scribbles down the name,
    then looks pensive.
Roxanne . o O (??)
Valentine would like another . . . hint, but
    not about poetry.
Roxanne . o O (?????)
Valentine says, "You read my post. I guess I
    should have realized you might read it. So
    you know I'm just coming out. And I was
    hoping to talk to you about it."
Roxanne says, "I see."

C.J.'s half-felt hopes for romance sagged. To
Valentine, she was just a information source. She
stared cynically at the screen and for a long minute,
Valentine didn't say anything.

Valentine says, "I've offended you."
Roxanne says, "Well, it wasn't exactly false
    pretenses."
Valentine exclaims, "Really, it wasn't! I do
    love poetry and I am adding lesbian poets
    to my library at an incredible pace. But I
    also thought who better to tell me what I
    want to know than a lesbian who likes poetry
    too."
Roxanne . o O (I wonder what she really wants
    to know?)
Valentine whispers "Tell me what my first time
    with a woman will be like" to Roxanne.

"Holey moley," C.J. said. She shivered — what a challenge!

> Roxanne says, "I can't tell you what it'll
> feel like when you first sleep with a woman.
> I can only tell you what it felt like to
> me."
> Valentine smiles. "That would be . . .
> perfect."
> Roxanne studies Valentine's face. "I'll send
> you an e-mail."
> Roxanne has disconnected.

C.J. put on her reading glasses and reached for her Thesaurus. Perhaps the chance for romance wasn't dead after all. She would write something that would captivate Valentine. And keep her coming back for more.

> To: valentine@intouch.com
> My nerves vibrated to hers. My eyes saw only
> her hand, slowly reaching toward my forearm.
> When she touched it my skin trembled and I
> felt pierced, like I'd had a shot, and it
> was an arrow straight to my sex. I should
> say to my heart, I know, but this moment
> wasn't about my heart.
> It was about her lips, so similar to my own,
> soft and pale mauve, inclining toward mine.
> I knew they would be gentle and even then
> I was not prepared for the whisper of their
> touch.
> I was a cauldron below, and my ache for her
> fingers kept time with my pounding heart.

I heard nothing but the sounds she made as
   she kissed me.
She was gentle for those first few minutes,
   our kisses languid and heady. I lay back
   in her arms and I swear I felt the world
   turning under me.
Then I was aware of being on the edge of the
   world. Sitting still I felt the speed of
   it turning. Held on the planet not by
   gravity, but by her arms. Wind seemed to
   tear through my hair and I took her hands,
   and put them on my breasts, and begged her
   to tear me open to my very heart and make
   me more a woman than I'd ever been before.
She pressed me down and her hands found their
   way under my clothes. I thought my breasts
   would burst, they were so hard and full and
   aching toward her mouth.
I had never been so needy or so ready and I've
   never again been that demanding. I was
   incapable of thinking of her needs at that
   time. I needed her, in me, in me now, in
   me quickly and faster and deeper and I was
   beyond sound and color and reason.
Her fingers in me, then her mouth on me. Then
   fulfillment, finally. For a few minutes.

To: roxanne@womanwire.com
You didn't describe what it felt like making
   love to her.

C.J. grinned. Valentine was hooked.

* * * * *

To: valentine@intouch.com

I remember that when I finally came back to myself, back in her bedroom, she still had her head on my thigh and slowly, like a drop of rain on a window, her tongue wandered over my swollen, still hungry flesh. It was so knowing and so intimate. I moaned and knew I was wet again.

She sat up, her face painted with me and satisfaction. She asked me if I liked that and I said couldn't she tell? She asked me if I wanted her in me again and I said couldn't she tell? Soon then, she said, but I told her I couldn't wait.

Her fingers, still wet with me, teased my nipples and I spread myself on the bed, gasping. I was so hungry for her.

She knelt on the bed next to me and I looked for the first time at her thighs, at the dark, silken triangle above them.

Hunger fled. I was thirsty. And I begged her again. This time to let me taste her. I pulled her knees apart and struggled on my back to get between them, I raised my mouth to her . . .

There is no secret. I loved finding what would make her moan loudest. I exulted in the power to make her cry out and shudder as I had. Time, patience and loving it, every second.

When she begged me, between her ragged gasps, to taste her again, I knew I had done it right.

* * * * *

```
To: roxanne@womanwire.com
You take my breath away.
You have been so generous to me that I hesitate
    to ask for further advice, but I will anyway.
I first began to doubt my heterosexuality
    because of a lesbian at work. I am burning
    for this woman. I have tried every way I
    can think of to make her look at me, see
    me as a woman she can desire, right down
    to    shamelessly    letting    my    blouse
    "accidentally" unbutton. I can't think
    about the future, only the present. Only a
    today that ends with her in my bed.
If you were this woman, what would it take for
    me to seduce you?
```

C.J. studied the last message from Valentine, depressed to the maximum. So much for romance. Valentine was already hooked on someone else. She had stayed up almost all night composing her first message and had functioned far below her usual standards at work. Fortunately, Lisa had seemed too tired to notice.

She had sent the e-mail and then waited a few minutes, just in case. Sure enough, Valentine's response had come almost immediately — she had obviously stayed up all night, too.

So last night, C.J. had come home from work and spent the rest of the evening on the second message, until she thought the screen was bobbing up and down, then realized it was her head that was bobbing. It had all been for nothing because

Valentine just wanted advice on how to seduce some woman at work.

She didn't have any inspiration for Valentine. She'd never thought about seducing anyone at work. At that moment, into her sleep-deprived mind, an image of Lisa intruded. C.J. realized she wanted to take Lisa from behind the shelf and into the busy room of her life.

She chided herself for her inconstancy. Was it Valentine or Lisa who intrigued her imagination? Lisa was a real, breathing woman, Valentine a persona. Lisa and Valentine both shared C.J.'s love of poetry and words. And didn't Lisa have season tickets to the opera, which was C.J.'s other great love? Lisa was witty and charming, but so was Valentine. Valentine was a lesbian. Lisa was straight.

Setting aside her motives, she decided the following night to answer Valentine's message. She got off to a good start and didn't question that in her mind's eye, Valentine had smoky-gray eyes and elegant hands.

> To: valentine@intouch.com
> If I were that woman, here's what might take me by surprise and in my surprise, make me vulnerable to your powers of persuasion.
> Lure me to work late with you, so late that everyone has gone home. The janitor has come and gone and all the lights are low except for the one burning at my desk. Step out of the darkness, startle me.
> Startle me with your leather jacket unzipped so I can see enough of you to be taken aback, enough to make me look again, and

```
        yearn for the naked breasts I can almost
        but not quite see.
    Will you approach me and draw my mouth to your
        breasts, letting the shock of my touch make
        you even bolder? Will you shed your jacket
        and straddle my lap, giving me your- self,
        demanding that I feast? How will you shape
        that first time with me?
```

C.J. hesitated, her fingers poised even as her inspiration flickered and died. "This is never going to happen," she said to herself. "I'm just fooling myself. There just isn't any point." She pressed one last key. "Sorry Valentine."

```
    Entry discarded.
    Roxanne has disconnected.
```

Although she longed to go home and go to sleep, C.J. found herself working late again. Lisa had asked so nicely that she'd said yes. And on a Friday night, but then if she wasn't working what would she be doing? Sitting at home, thinking about Valentine and feeling guilty she'd never responded to Valentine's last message though her mind had played out how she would love Lisa to seduce her, over and over again. Home was no escape.

The later she stayed at work the more time she spent with Lisa. Lisa had seemed preoccupied these last few days, but that didn't stop C.J. from noticing that today Lisa was wearing jeans that had shrunk to fit her like a glove. She told herself she shouldn't be thinking about someone she worked with that way. Certainly not a straight someone. But Lisa tended to stand so close that C.J. could sense her body heat. Lisa's hand on her shoulder had left a steamy imprint that C.J. felt hours later.

It just wasn't fair.

She realized the floor was almost dark and she called out, "How's it going, Lisa?"

C.J. jumped when Lisa's voice came back just outside her cubicle. "I'm going to call it quits. I have other things on my mind."

Something made C.J. look up from her screen as Lisa leaned in the partition doorway. Her breath caught and she stared.

Lisa stepped toward her and the low light glinted on the zipper of her leather jacket. "Waiting for you to figure it out is taking too long. So I'm just going to put myself on the line." She slowly pulled the tab on the zipper lower. "You're dense, you know that?"

C.J. tried to lower the zipper further with the sheer force of her gaze. She managed to croak out, "Valentine?" She sounded as stupid as she felt.

"In the flesh."

And how. C.J. swallowed. "But I didn't tell you how to seduce me. So how did you know?"

"Have I seduced you?" Lisa stepped toward her.

C.J. was speechless.

Lisa unzipped the jacket all the way.

Those Who Can't Do

Melissa Hartman

After a week of my undeniable and apparently very baffling rejection of your advances, you gratefully accompany me as I wait in line to deposit my paycheck. You can't imagine what you did to provoke my anger, and then what miracle forces beyond your comprehension have worked toward its retraction; yet, here we stand. You don't inquire. That we are together again — even under the most mundane circumstances — is enough for you.

You still have no idea why last Monday I refused

your offer to assist me in photocopying class materials in the faculty copy room. "I'm simply not in the mood for your company," propels you from my side as surely as if you've been hit by a round from a assault rifle. You are wearing a leather jacket, the one I told you looks so handsome on you; you wear it more frequently these days. I walk on to the copy room with one of the women's volleyball coaching assistants. You and she have a great deal in common. In her I see a pronounced tendency that for you has become an obsession.

On Tuesday afternoon you show up at my office, presumably to see if my mood has mellowed. It has not. You believe I have no knowledge of your present emotional turmoil. Surprise. The way you feel now is the price one pays for loving too well, and not at all wisely. And here is something more to add to your pain: I order you out because I am expecting a student for a private conference regarding her eligibility for the Sophomore Essay Prize, the honor you covet, you assume, secretly. I am chain smoking Kents, and blow some smoke in your direction for your benefit. You stifle a cough as you leave.

When I arrive at eight o'clock on Wednesday morning, you are already waiting for me in the dark bank of offices. I feel your breath on the back of my neck as I bend to place the key in the lock.

"May I help you?" Your voice is gentle with hope. Others might soften at hearing it.

Instead I feign lack of recognition, and shock, and somehow manage to emit an undignified yelp of what I intend for you to take as fear.

You are solicitous of perhaps having caused me even a moment's distress. "Have I startled you? I'm

sorry." Oh, your gallantry is only surpassed by your
need to please!

"Don't sneak up behind me!" I command,
sounding ragged after a night of Kents, after a night
of watching a *woman* — Corinne — sleeping on the
pillow next to mine. All these years, and the
improbability of the situation still astounds me.

"I don't sneak!" This I know well, but you fail to
recognize that honesty is not always best. Your voice,
however, could lure the queen of the Nile away from
Antony, even though it has little effect on me. You
steal a moment in the darkness before I flick on the
fluorescent lights of my office to ask, "At least tell
me what I've done *now*, Rita. What was it?"

The best time to pay for such brashness is
immediately. "If you don't know, take a few days to
think about it. In the meantime, leave me alone!"

You back away stricken, a stray and starving cat
I've kicked for begging the food of love from me. You
retreat so quickly your stringy blonde hair flies
behind you. I idly wonder if you have left off
shampooing for want of my attention.

In the year since you appeared, moon-faced,
sullen, and gifted, in my freshman composition class,
you've never declared your infatuation to me. I prefer
it that way. I'm able to amuse myself with the
effects of it, and I reserve the option of pretending
that it doesn't exist. I'll never have to hear how
much I mean to you, or how you'll spend the rest of
your life reconciling yourself to the fact that I never
would sleep with you. One day you'll realize the favor
I did you. Unrequited love — especially unrequited
first love — is a character builder.

During this year, you have written a series of love

poems, inspired in the classical manner by an unobtainable and unidentified love object. A gratifying theme: It makes for a prolific output. Your poems are compelling for someone your age, but not sufficiently memorable to quote now, although I can quite easily recall some of my written commentary about them: "What a unique perspective! It is plain that you can write!" I gushed across your pages. I meant only at first to encourage your literary ambition. As your writing instructor, that is one of the things I do. But I soon discerned that your greater talent lies in loving, particularly in loving me, so that is what I seek to bring out in you. You will learn more in your fruitless pursuit of me than with all your delight in Shakespeare and Keats. I cringe with embarrassment over your sincerity and giggle with Corinne at your naïveté. Oh no one can take a crumb and fish the ocean with it quite like you!

You are a talented student, able to withstand my tests of devotion in a positively commendable way. Last year I found your class frighteningly unresponsive to Muriel Spark's *The Prime of Miss Jean Brodie* and its unique exploration of the life-or-death influence a teacher can have on her students. I think, although its warning fell on your deaf ears, nevertheless you saw my method laid out, and in a most admirable form. I considered it worthwhile to show you the frosty sensuality Maggie Smith brings to the title role, and I screened the movie version for you and twenty of your bored classmates. Afterward, smoldering with checked passion, you rolled the VCR cart back to the audiovisual room for me. I now had gained your permission where before I had ravaged unauthorized. Many of your subsequent poems remarked on this fact; others bemoaned it.

Of course, the difficulties that you are having with me this week are of a completely different caliber. I have no doubt, however, that you'll be able to come through just fine — providing you display the necessary fortitude.

You are nineteen, and I am thirty-five, on the brink of middle age and none too pleased at finding myself here. That you doted openly was at first to your credit. Then I taught you restraint, not to attempt to speak to me after each class, nor to attend my every office hour; it was then that I began to reward you with my attention.

As always, it's a seller's market. And you hold out for more than most — squiring me to a dental appointment, to union headquarters to file a grievance, to the grocery to shop for delicacies to tempt Corinne's sluggish appetite after a nasty tournament with the flu. You crave whatever time I can spare you. I don't mind this kind of greed in you.

Over the summer break, you became aware of the impact my absence can have on your life. That first day of the fall semester you spent more than four hours helping me assemble my course materials. You were jubilant. You showed the appreciation of a drowning woman for air.

You know I live with Corinne. I think this has been keeping your hopes high that someday, somehow, you and I, if only . . . Yet you have no way of knowing that Corinne and I were lovers for just the first few years of our twelve together, that although we still share a bed, we are not intimate.

Disapproval seemed to thump at me from every pair of eyes I glanced into, and being well thought of has always been important to me. You cannot know that over the years Corinne has reconciled herself to our conditional existence together and, I think, has not had the easiest time doing so.

I find you rather bold — and entertaining — in your desire of me. Perhaps you may even have plans of waiting for me until Corinne dies. You have met her, and know that she is more than twenty-five years my senior, and not young for those years. You, however young in years, possess an old soul, a soul that must be appalled by your so complete and so futile love for me.

Though your little remark about what you have done "now" may indicate that we hold differing views on this point, I think that this week when I haven't permitted you to see me has been the first time I have overtly attempted to make you suffer. Wouldn't you like to know why?

The offense you so innocuously committed was openly reading *The Well of Loneliness* while waiting for me in the hallway outside my office last Friday. Any number of my colleagues could have passed — and most likely did — in front of you so devotedly waiting outside my door; their eyes could not have failed to notice you reading that classic of lesbian literature while expecting me for a personal appointment. You chose the one title recognizable even to those who think, as did Queen Victoria, that women can't experience "the love that dare not speak its name." You have to understand that your love for me is to remain undeclared not only to me, but to my peers. Oh, I'm sure they suspect a crush, but for them to know how large it looms for you, and the extent to which I tolerate it, might result in their misunderstanding of the place I accord it in my daily routine.

Get used to the idea that you will spend your life hiding your books and your feelings, or you will not spend another minute of it around me.

Today — Friday — when I pass you in the hall and invite you to come with me while I deposit my paycheck, you hesitate before leaving the gaggle of young men and women you are talking with. Obviously you haven't expected reconciliation so soon. Your eyes won't meet mine, but your relief at my relenting is palpable.

It is a brilliantly sunny day, with sharp, shocking bursts of wind that steal the words from my mouth. You observe a stony silence — further evidence that you are unprepared for me to be so amiable — while I carry on a monologue as we drift down Lexington Avenue to the bank. I regale you with an account of some student's supposedly brilliant *Grapes of Wrath* essay, turn my ankle purposely so that you have to catch me by my erring elbow. For some reason, however, I find this gallantry irritating just now. You accept yourself so graciously. You are fine with it. Well, someone has to show you the folly of such composure. If this is the way you are going to love, see now what it is all about. As we stand in that crowded line at the bank, I ask, "Do you want to know what made me so angry?"

"What was it, Rita?" You sound weary, and this displeases me. You don't seem to comprehend the severity of your breach of our private etiquette. And when I inform you: "Rita, I can read what I like," is not reassuring. Certainly you realize that you need to be with me no matter what my terms. Why don't you admit it? I must make you feel the danger of what you've done. I raise my voice to make certain the twenty-five or so people around us can hear.

"I don't know if you're a lesbian," I declare definitively, watching you cringe as the heads of the workaday slaves swivel to focus on you, "but I'm *not.*"

You stand in the spotlight of their stares as a calm seems to settle over you, or is it coldness? Of all things, you smile. You don't look pleased, but you smile. "Of course not, you can't be. What was I thinking?" Your voice is clear and even. Without another word or glance, you leave my side and walk out toward the sunny street. Before you've exited the revolving door, I am aware that the eyes of the others in line have turned on me.

Let them look. This is obviously one lesson you're not ready to learn.

Backseat Driver

Robbi Sommers

We're sitting in the dance club. My best girl, her two friends, and I huddle around the small table. The room is dark and smoky. The dance floor is packed. The DJ's beat is hard and sexual. I ride the rhythm. Music wraps inside of me and tightens me down like a coiled spring. I'm tense and ready to shoot. Knocking back vodka — not a drinker but don't care — tonight, I'm looking for the edge.

My best girl watches every move I make. Her

hawk eyes miss nothing. Once, she pressed me into a doorway and made me come just by staring me down. Tonight, she's looking at me like that — like she might push me until she gets me off with her eyes.

I'm thinking about movement. If I sashay across the room — give her a glimpse of my want-it-now kind of a walk — will she follow me out to the cool night and into the backseat of my friend's car? Can I tempt her to give me my way or will she stay smooth and aloof until she's ready? She takes pleasure in working her charms. Her specialty is the sting of desire, and she orchestrates passion like a maestro. I sit across the table and wait for direction.

Her friends toast, and we clink our glasses. My girl's face is unreadable, but I scan her eyes for clues. Desperate for the chance, I wrestle the urge to strut the room to get my way. Someone said something funny? My girl laughs then glances at me. The heat from her expression sears me, brands me, makes me remember how much of me she holds in the palm of her hand. I squirm in my chair. God, have I ever known a woman as hot as her?

I want it now, can barely wait. We're an hour from home. Why had we thought riding with friends was a good idea? Held hostage until we're dropped off, I'm suddenly aware that this night may be way too long.

"Have to pee," I whisper in her ear and rise. Will she watch me cross the room? I'll move like a siren. I'll leave a mist of steam behind that intoxicates. She'll have no choice but to come after me.

I step back from the table, but she grabs my arm. "No, you don't," she says, her tone steady. A speculative smile follows her words.

"I don't?" I reciprocate with a flirty pout.

She shakes her head and tugs my arm until I have no choice but to sit back down. She pulls my chair and draws me close to her.

"This isn't about peeing, is it?" she whispers in my ear. "This is about you wanting something else, right?"

I nod but say nothing.

"And we both know that, bottom line, you like waiting."

I nod again. Bottom line? I hate/love waiting, but she makes me suffer so sweet — and in reality, what choice do I have? Jerk back up and insist that I'm going to the restroom? Flaunt the walk, play the odds, hope she'll come after me in a wild fury? Take me down in the hallway? In the alley? In the car? A master, she keeps me on the brink. If I stand up now and walk the room, she'll simply watch me for a moment then turn her head as if unaffected. I know her. I know her well.

She snakes her arms around my waist and I lean into her.

"You know what I have planned for you?" Her warm breath teases my ear. "I'm going to please you tonight. Would you like that?"

I nod.

"Would you like that, Sweetheart? Do you like how I pay close attention to you? How I'm always one step ahead?"

I keep nodding — with her, I have no reason to stop.

"Later, after I've made you so, so ready, I'm going to take you all the way down, make you whimper in exquisite pleasure. You want that, don't you?"

Her slinky words spiral around me in shimmering waves. Dizzy from anticipation, drunk on her promise, I continue to nod. A blue light blinks intermittently above the dance floor. Red and yellow light beams weave then disengage. Like the lights on the ceiling, like the shot of vodka, her whispered words sharpen the edge. I clench and unclench my fist. My breath has quickened. When I shift slightly in the chair, the pressure against my clit kneads and excites.

"And there's no hurry, is there? There's plenty of time. We have all of tonight, don't we, Sweetheart?" She pulls back slightly, turns to my friend, and motions to me. "You should see how hot she gets after she has to wait."

"I'd like to." The friend flashes me a seductive look.

"Oh, God —" Flustered, I move haphazardly, knocking the friend's drink all over the table. "Oh, Jesus — Oh, God —" My face heats with a flush, and I hurry to the restroom to regroup? to hide? No one follows me. Good.

I stare at my reflection in the mirror. Would my girl want her friend to watch? Was this the surprise for the night? Would they barge into the restroom and push me into a stall? One props me up while the other fucks me hard?

But no one comes through the restroom door.

Where are they? Instinctively, I take the lipstick from my pocket and re-tint my lips. I fluff my hair and unbutton a crucial button on my shirt, but no one comes through that door.

The music pulsates from somewhere beyond — out there — where they are. I know her. She's at the table, making some plans, taking care of business in that polished way of hers. I should make her wait. Haven't they wondered when I'm coming back? Yeah, make her wait. I lean against the sink and count to ten, to twenty, to thirty, and on — and no one comes through the restroom door.

I slip the lipstick in my pocket, grab a handful of paper towels, and head for the table — after all, the night is young and the table must be soaked.

We're on the dance floor. My girl wears men's cologne — DK. *Fuel for men* — and the fragrance swirls from her in a thin breeze. She moves like she's burning some kind of untamed energy, all right. She's volatile, a time bomb — any moment the subtle ticking could discharge into passion. Focused on me, only on me, she sways. The beat is seductive. The beat is erotic. The beat is relentless. I can't imagine holding out until we're home. Can I get her out to the car?

I look her in the eyes and smile. I dance like I'm a call girl, paid to please with movement. She looks too good. She has me, and I can hardly breathe. I fight the urge to pull her hand to my thickened nipple. I struggle with the compulsion to force her fingers into my sex.

A vamp, I dance around her. A temptress, I brush my breasts against hers. I'm thinking about being taken. I'm contemplating her strong hands all over me. Sweat and cologne — a sex-driving mix — all I can think of is her scent when she fucks me.

I grab her and shoot fast, hot words into her ear. "Let's go to the car." I kiss her ear. I lick her neck. If she wanted, she could take me right on this dance floor. On that table. Against the bar. I don't care.

She pulls back and laughs. She's happy. She's pleased. She spins in a circle and comes back to me. She says something but I can't hear, what with that driving, nonstop beat.

"What?" I raise my hands in a questioning gesture.

She stops dancing and just stares at me. Not a smile, not a twinkle in the eyes, just a cool, slick stare. I don't move. I stand in front of her and wait. Her hands come to my face and she leans so close, so deliciously close that I am engulfed in her. Slow, easy, she kisses me. Her lips are soft and warm, and I feel as if I am swimming in dark clouds. She teases her tongue on my lips and, without hesitation, I grant her entry. With her kiss, she has stopped the music, the movement, the lights. We sink into the abyss of lust. We burrow deep into a place where there's nothing but her and me.

"I'm ready to leave," she says, her lips still pressed to mine.

I simply nod.

* * * * *

They're in the front seat, we're in the back. The radio is blaring, Nina Simone. The Jeep's cruising — maybe sixty, maybe seventy — down the freeway. It's raining and the friend forges through large puddles in the road.

"We're going way too fast," I say nervously in my girl's ear.

She squeezes my hand and leans to the front seat. "Slow down."

The driver automatically backs off the gas. My girl puts her arm around me and pulls me closer. "Okay now?" I nod. We splash through another pool of water and almost swerve into the guardrail.

"Maybe you should move out of the fast lane," my girl says loud to her friend.

"Backseat driver?" the friend calls to us.

My girl laughs and pulls me closer. I love how she takes care of me.

"You want to know what I'd like to do? Right here? Right now?" my girl says in my ear.

"What?" I mutter.

"I'd like to lean you back in this seat and suck on your pussy."

A hard throb ignites my clit. "Oh yeah?" I say, but I'm not sure she's heard me because she's talking before I finish the sentence.

"I'd like to take down your pants and get those sweet legs of yours on my shoulders . . . bury my face right in your pussy, right here, right now."

"Hey, you talking behind my back about my driving?" The driver twists the rearview mirror. The passenger turns toward us.

"You want to know what I'm talking about?" My girl takes her arm from around me and grabs the back of the front seat.

"Backseat driver," the friend taunts.

"What I'm taking about —" My girl glances at me with a smug look and turns back to her friends. "is how I'd like to eat her pussy right here in the back of this car. Right?" She turns to me. "Wasn't that what I was saying?" Her focus shifts to the front.

"Oh, God —" I grab her thigh. My face is immediately warm. She's embarrassed me again. *Eat her pussy?* Since when does she talk like some street-corner thug? *Eat her pussy right here in the back of this car.* Well, yes, I could see some sort of a scene with her friend . . . but right here? In such a small space? Within seconds the entire car would smell like pussy — *my* pussy. I cringe. I hope she's teasing and squeeze her thigh again to retrieve her attention.

She doesn't look at me. Instead she leans forward and perches between her friends. "Would you mind? Would you care if I went down on her right now?" She's talking real loud now.

"Not me," says the passenger, the very friend who was so willing to watch how hot waiting made me get.

The driver shrugs. "Only if I'm allowed to go over fifty-five." She laughs. They all laugh.

I pull my girl back to me. "We can't," I whisper desperately. "The car will smell like my pussy."

She leans back to her friends. "She's worried the car will smell like her pussy. Anyone here mind?"

Oh, oh God.

"Not me." The passenger has twisted in her seat.

"Not me." The driver's eyes gleam in the rearview mirror.

"Feel free to watch," my girl says. "She likes to be watched. Don't you, Sweetheart?"

"Yes, but —" I hate to be a party poop, but I can't seem to get past the pussy/car thing.

"Lie back." My girl's got that serious tone. She's peering at me with those cool, dark eyes.

"Really, I think we should —" I want to persuade her to reconsider, but she cuts me off in an instant.

"Lie back," she insists.

This is the part that I hate. This is the part that I love. I could say no. Stare right at her and say that simple word. *No.* That's all it would take. As much as I want to, as much as the idea of everyone crammed in this Jeep breathing my pussy makes me feel vulnerable and inhibited, *no* seems out of reach. I lie back.

She's on me in a second — kissing me, talking in my ear. "Oh baby, yes, baby. I'll take care of you so, so sweet. You know it. You know it, don't you." She's all over me. Her fingers are quick, and my shirt unbuttons in record time. She tugs the bra cup down and pinches my already hard nipple.

"Jesus, baby. Sweetheart. Honey." She unbuckles my belt, unzips my pants, and struggles to get them over my hips. The passenger is watching every move my girl makes. In the mirror, the driver's eyes shift erratically from road to mirror, road to mirror. The car sails down the freeway — forty? fifty? sixty? seventy? — it's hard to tell. Seems fast. Seems slow.

I lift my ass. I help my girl pull my trousers down, past my knees. Someone turns down the music. Someone sighs. The car seems alive. Its breath is long and laborious.

"Yes, oh yes," someone whispers as my panties slip down my thighs.

My girl lifts my legs and pushes between them. I close my eyes. All I can hear is that nonstop breath and the swish-swosh of the windshield wipers.

"I'm going to have your pussy," my girl says.

"Yes, oh yes," someone whispers again.

"Suck your clit. Your meaty, pulpy clit."

I peek. My girl guides the passenger's hand to my breast. My girl then dips her face into my pussy, leaving the passenger to do as she pleases with my nipple. The passenger seems pleased to be included. Immediately, with a vigorous pinch, she vise-grips the erect flesh.

On reflex, I snap at her arm, grab the flesh between my teeth and bite. And my girl, oh my girl, is buried between my pussy lips. Her tongue laps and flicks at my bead. My clit feels bloated, full-blown, ready to pop.

And the car — the car keeps breathing in and out, in and out in that prolonged, weighty breath.

It's good. It's so good. My girl slides her heated tongue along my ribbed, thick opening and figure-eights her way back to the clit-bulb. Slides down to the slit. Glides back to the tiny marble. Again and again.

The pleasure is intense and I gasp — only to realize that the entire car smells like one thing, and one thing only —

Oh, oh, God.

My girl sinks her fingers into my cunt and starts to fuck me in that way, that juicy, juicy way that

creates that loud slapping sound. The car breathes
in a drawn-out inhalation/exhalation. Swish-swosh.
Swish-swosh. The wipers compete with the buttery
smacking sound of her palm against my lips.

There's pussy everywhere. The seat beneath me is
drenched. My thighs are damp. My wetness sprinkles
from her uncompromising hand to my belly and only
God knows where else.

"God, you smell good," my girl mutters. She pulls
her fingers from between my legs. "Want to smell?"
She offers her hand to the passenger who releases
my nipple and takes the hand.

"Oh, yes." She inhales deeply. "Oh, yes." She runs
her tongue across the cream-covered fingers.

"Car smells like pussy, all right," the driver adds.

Swish-swosh. Swish-swosh. My girl has her fingers
back in my slit. She's driving me now. She's going
nonstop, and I'm on the edge of a good cum. The
Jeep's flying down the freeway — eighty? ninety? one
hundred? — and I'm hanging on to keep from floating
to the ceiling and out some open vent. The
passenger's got my nipple again. My girl's fucking me
and working my clit simultaneously. I'm on the
climb. I'm racing toward the top of the cliff and off
into space. *Swish-swosh. Swish-swosh.*

She's got me. She's got me good. And we're going
too, too fast. Someone going to slow this thing down?
I'm there. I'm riding a good cum now. She's twisting
my nipple, she's whipping my clit, she's slap-fucking
me, and I can't stay on this seat any more . . .

"Hey," my girl says. She leans to the front. I'm

in a stupor but well aware that all of us smell like my pussy. "You missed our exit."

"Shit." The driver veers her eyes back to the road. "Where the hell are we?"

My girl — backseat driver that she is — leans back with a smirk and proceeds to inform us exactly where we are and . . .

where we're going next.

Paris

Pat Welch

It sailed through the air, a soft white sphere, a
dot on the blue sky. I watched as the softball floated
somewhere over the scruffy trees that edged the
sandy field.

"Good one!" someone shouted from the bleachers.
The ball finally landed out of sight just past the
fence. Spatters of applause broke through the muggy
air of late afternoon. The heat shimmered in a
nimbus that encircled the girl running around the
bases. I kept my eyes on her as she ran home.

Next to me, Rhonda shifted on the grass. "It's late," she said as she stood up and stretched. I kept my eyes on the game, away from her tanned arms and legs, her short blonde hair that curled at the edge of the white cotton shirt all the recreation supervisors wore. I looked up only when she leaned over and peered into my face, her white teeth gleaming in her brown face.

"Want to help me straighten up the rec room?" I nodded, struggled my clumsy body from the ground, and followed her. The heat struck with all its usual intensity. After sitting still so long I felt as if I were moving through water, with all the sights and sounds of the familiar school playgrounds distorted in a greenish haze.

Not for the first time, as I trudged away from the softball field, I marveled at the strange combination of events that had given me a chance to meet Rhonda. She was in the midst of earning a degree at Florida State, up in Gainesville. Working as a recreation supervisor here in a tightly enclosed suburb of Miami and being a glorified baby-sitter for the children of working parents was only a stepping stone for Rhonda. As soon as summer was over she was off to France, for a whole year. I'd heard her speak French a few times, listening to the way the fluid sounds rolled inside her mouth and spilled off her tongue.

"Storm coming." she said over her shoulder. I looked up at the sky. The black edge of rain was visible in the east. Every day in August, at about four o'clock, the skies opened with a roar, fizzing lightning and shattering the heavy silence with rain

and thunder. Half an hour later, the sun would glare
down again, steaming the water into the air before it
had a chance to soak into the sandy soil.

Our shadows fell across each other as we hurried
to the rec room where it bulged out from the
elementary school building, a weird excrescence of
yellow concrete stuck on a gray monolith. Rhonda
held the door open for me as I lumbered behind her,
ashamed of my size and clumsiness. After all these
weeks I still couldn't figure out why she took any
interest in me. She was so graceful, so pretty, so
popular — everything I wasn't. How could I, an
ignorant and awkward teenager, silent and withdrawn, rate her attention?

My family had moved only a year ago from a
small town in Mississippi to Palm Valley, a flat, dull
conglomeration of square houses surrounded by
swampland that had only recently been tamed by
miles of paving for the new freeway system. At first
I'd been confused. How could they call it a valley
when, so far as I could tell, the entire state of
Florida was as flat as a pancake? I gave up trying to
figure it out and accepted it as just another of those
strange double meanings that made up my world.

Unfortunately, my thick accent had immediately
marked me as surely as the brand of Cain, singling
me out for ridicule and disgust among my peers. So
did my hand-me-down clothes, inherited from a
variety of relatives. So did my familiarity with the
Bible and with hellfire and brimstone and tent
meetings. So did my fondness for odd foods,
deep-fried and thick with sweetness.

* * * * *

"You have to go to the recreation program at the school this summer," Daddy had said with that stare that meant I'd get slapped across the room if I protested. "Your mother has to go to work for a few months." He'd forced the words out as Mother set his food on the table. As he spoke, he looked down at his plate, loaded with meatloaf and potatoes, and directed his pronouncements at the food he was about to consume.

"But, Daddy, I'm fifteen now. I'm old enough to stay at home. I can take care of myself."

His stare moved up to my face, and I felt the words withering in the air between us. "That's right," he'd said in the quiet tone that I secretly called the Voice of Doom, the voice that scared me more than if he'd been yelling at me. "You're fifteen. Just the right age to get in trouble."

He meant boys. Hah. If only he knew how all the boys in my acquaintance, even the boys at church, did their best to avoid me. I kept waiting to be upset about that fact, but I was relieved, though I never let anyone know that. I glanced at my mother, who was calmly gnawing on an ear of corn. It was better at that moment, I knew, not to bring up how she'd run off and married my father when she was sixteen. I also knew something else — that the job at the new mall had been a small, hard-won victory for her.

So we all sat quietly, listening to the television in the background as it blurted out the news of our troops leaving Vietnam. I accepted all of it: the news, my mother's struggles, the sentence of sports and games and enforced hilarity with strangers that I was to endure for three months. It was just like the knowledge that we lived in Palm Valley, which was

completely flat, contained very few palms, and was
enclosed not by hills but by paved six-lane highways.

The shock of cool air from the rec room jarred
me from my reverie. Rhonda put her hands on her
hips and looked around with a sigh. "Just look at
this mess," she muttered. Ping-pong balls and paddles
were splayed over the rickety, dented green table that
teetered against the wall. A croquet set had been
tossed just inside the entrance, and I nearly tripped
over a mallet that fell as the door slammed behind
us. Someone had left a board game — it looked like
Clue — scattered on one of the Formica tables that
lined the room.

We worked in silence for a few minutes, picking
up, shoving into cupboards, pulling into alignment.
Rain pounded with a sudden roar on the flat roof.
Rhonda turned to me and we smiled at each other at
our close escape from a thorough drenching. Our
isolation was complete.

"Where is everybody?"

She shrugged. "I guess the softball team ran to
the gym. Everybody probably just ran for cover
wherever they could."

"I guess so." I saw Rhonda twinge with pain as
she lifted a chair toward a table. "Does your shoulder
still hurt?"

"Damn thing won't quit!" She reached her other
arm around to massage the tender spot where neck
and shoulder met while I stared, unable to look
away. "Maybe I'll put a heating pad on it tonight."

I walked up behind her as she sat down with a

sigh in the chair she'd moved. "Do you think you
should see a doctor?" I fretted. "You hurt yourself
last week."

She shook her head and leaned her elbows on the
table. "Oh, it's nothing, just overdid it, that's all."

Facing her back, I felt brave enough to go on.
"You shouldn't have spent so much time working
with me. I don't think I'll ever be any good at
softball or basketball or volleyball or any other kind
of ball," I said, finishing with a lame laugh as I
recalled how Rhonda had loped beside me for weeks
while I fumbled through the motions of all the
activities that came so easily to everyone else.

"Sure you will. You just need a little help."

I moved closer, suddenly on the verge of tears.
Who would help me when summer was over? "When
do you leave?" I asked.

"Next week," she sighed, leaning back in her
chair. "Then a whole semester in Paris." She turned
slightly, stiff from favoring the sore muscles. "Do you
remember any of the French I taught you?"

I laughed. "All I remember is that phrase from
the song — the one by Patti Labelle — 'voulez-vous
couchez avec moi.'"

She started laughing with me, and together we
sang the line, Rhonda still sitting in the chair and
drumming her palms on the table, me snapping my
fingers and dancing behind her. Without thinking,
without worrying, I put my hands on her shoulders.
She was still giggling as my fingers searched for the
pain.

"Is this where it hurts?" I asked softly.

"Lower." We were both silent now. My hands
kneaded the flesh, absorbing its warmth and firmness.

Her head dropped down and she moaned, the sound barely audible over the rain. I bent over to look at her face. Rhonda's eyes were wide open, and somehow I knew she was thinking exactly what I was thinking — that at any moment someone would walk in and we'd have to explain. I didn't quite know what we'd have to explain but I knew it would be uncomfortable.

"Do you want me to stop?"

"No. No, chérie." When she whispered the words I went all hot and cold at the same time. My skin savored her skin, as if I could somehow taste it. It was everything all rolled into one, all the things I'd tried to feel with boys and couldn't, the confusion and loneliness at how hopelessly different I was, the way I secretly raged at the silence that covered me like deep snow.

I'm not sure how long I stood there, gently stroking her, before her own hands moved. They rested on mine as my fingers continued to probe her neck and shoulders. She let go as I moved my hands to stroke her hair, her warm cheeks, her forehead damp with sweat. Her hair brushed my chin as she leaned back into me, her weight pressing against my small, tender breasts. My heart pounded as I shakily unbuttoned her blouse enough to get at the sweetness trapped inside the rough white cotton.

"Does it still hurt?" I murmured as I reached to the warm swell of her breasts, daring only to touch the edges of her bra.

"Yes." Her word was a signal to continue, so I massaged a little harder. My legs trembled, and I felt warm moisture seeping between them. I didn't notice time, the storm, the ugliness of the room. All I knew was Rhonda — her smell that soaked the air, the look of her half-closed eyes, her quick breaths, her warmth and softness. Had I always been this hungry for something I hadn't been able to name until now?

I knelt on the concrete floor, which was still warm from the collected heat of years of hot summer days. My hands trembled and left her body. "I'm sorry," I whispered. I didn't know I was crying until my tears dropped silently to the floor. "I'm so sorry."

Rhonda got up from the chair and bent beside me. "Why?" she said. "There's nothing to be sorry for. Don't ever apologize for who you are." She pulled me to my feet as she spoke. Her hand stayed on my arm, clasping gently as I stood before her.

"I'll burn in hell. It's sick, it's a sin —"

"Stop. All of that's a lie, do you hear me?" Her face was close to mine as she looked into my eyes. "There's nothing wrong with you, nothing sinful about you."

I looked down, afraid to meet her eyes. We stood there silent for several moments. Her kiss shocked me, and I stopped crying. It was so gentle, so tender, so unlike the rough gropings and shovings of the few boys who had approached me. Rhonda cupped my face in her hands, her eyes watching me with an unreadable expression.

"Why did you do that?" I gasped.

Rhonda's smile pierced me like a tiny arrow of pain and pleasure in my heart. "I don't know."

This time I reached for her. When our tongues met I knew that I would melt in the sweet fire that flowed inside me. We touched each other lightly, cautiously, almost respectfully as our kiss lingered.

When the lights crackled and the room went

black, we sprang apart as if we'd both felt the electricity of the storm in our bodies. It must have been only seconds before the door slammed open and a soaked cluster of the younger kids tumbled in, shouting and hitting.

"The lights are out all over!" one of them hollered in delight. In the dim light I could see that Rhonda had already buttoned her blouse. The man who'd been herding the little kids was dressed in the same white cotton shirt and shorts that Rhonda wore. He rolled his eyes at Rhonda in exasperation at the wildness the storm had stirred up in their charges.

In all the noise, darkness and confusion, I don't know if Rhonda noticed when I slipped out. I didn't even feel the rain pelting my body as I slowly walked through the soggy fields to the street that would take me home. I had to do something — anything — so that I wouldn't explode. But what?

Then I got the idea. I didn't know how to explain it, but I just knew Rhonda would be worried about what had happened today. I pictured her back in the rec room, her head filled with fears. Maybe she could get into real trouble if anyone found out, which meant she would be scared I'd talk about it. And how would people understand that nothing bad had happened? How would someone like my father, or the school principal, or the other recreation supervisors, know that Rhonda had helped me, not hurt me? And how would Rhonda know that?

My plan was really simple — no trouble at all, really. After all, she was leaving in just a few days, so it was no big deal if I stayed at the library instead of going to school. I fished in the pockets of my shorts until I found the dollar my mother had given me for a snack from the vending machines. The rain was almost gone, dying away in light, scattered drops as I made it to the drugstore.

I found the card I wanted right away. It was blank inside, thank goodness — no soppy, sugary poem to mess up what I wanted to say. I borrowed a pen from the cashier and sat down on a bench outside. It was hot again, and I held the card carefully so I wouldn't sweat on it.

I studied the painting of the Eiffel Tower on the card and thought. What did I want to say, anyway? That I loved her — that I knew that what happened between us was private, not for others know — that I finally understood so many, many things. It was like the stories we read in Sunday school. I'd been seeing through a glass darkly. Or maybe it was like a miracle, where I'd been lame but now I could walk. Where I'd been dumb but now I could speak. The dull, flat town spread out ahead of me, strangely glowing in a soft, new light as the sun cleared the black clouds.

Finally, I wrote. After handing the pen back to the clerk, I hurried back to the schoolyard. Had she already left?

I was in luck. Her little red car was parked next to the gym under a palm tree; the sun had already dried the rain from the hood. I walked across the parking lot, glancing around to see if I was being watched.

The only other people in sight were a bunch of high-school guys smearing themselves with mud and grass playing touch football, completely unaware of my presence at the other end of the field. The window by the driver's seat of Rhonda's car was open a bit to let out the heat that would have been accumulating for hours. I could see the residue of raindrops gleaming on the steering wheel as I nudged the card through the window. It fell to the seat, Rhonda's name clearly visible in black ink on the creamy white envelope.

As I walked away from the car, I knew that Rhonda would understand why I didn't want to come back while she was still there. It would be easier at the library to think about what had happened. There, in the quiet and the cool conditioned air, I could treasure the day, remember each moment, each feeling, understand it all better. Besides, I thought with a sharp fleeting pain, I wasn't sure I could say good-bye to Rhonda when she left next week.

In my mind I went back over the words I had written:

"Merci beaucoup. Au revoir." Yes, they were just right. Le mot juste, no?

I wanted to be alone. I didn't want to listen to my father drone on about the problems with the world today. I didn't want to answer my mother's anxious questions about my activities and my nonexistent friends. Just for a little while, I wanted to be by myself.

I turned my steps off the street that led to my house and took the path that led to the canal that edged Palm Valley. It was almost overflowing after the rain. The force of the storm had cleaned the algae from its surface, and today it was a deep, clear green. You could see to the bottom now. Tiny fish, minnows maybe, scurried near the edge of the canal. I wondered what the Seine looked like, and I promised myself that one day I would find out.

The walk home would be a long one, I knew, but I didn't mind. It felt good to go a different way. I'd get there soon enough.

Hearts of Summer

Laura DeHart Young

The streets were quiet. The only sound she heard was the rhythmic cadence of her own footsteps hitting pavement as she jogged, circling the block where she lived like a vulture in the desert. It could've been the desert. It was only June, but it was hot.

The pavement began to incline sharply as she turned the corner onto her own street. Looking up the hill, she could see the dimly lit apartmont building. And on the porch, the soft glow of a cigarette. The woman had returned.

As she drew nearer, she glanced quickly at the woman's face. The shadowed features were there, then suddenly gone — left behind by her own systematic motion. It was a memorable face, one she'd stop to admire twice at the mall or the supermarket. Sharp, mature, thoughtful.

The woman had been watching her run every night for the last two weeks. She wanted to say hello, to introduce herself. But each evening, when the last lap ended, the woman was gone, the cement stoop empty of her shadow. She began to wonder if the image was a dream, some kind of specter that flickered alive and then dimmed within the confines of her own imagination.

Until tonight. Tonight she'd decided to run one less lap. Decided to stop before the mysterious woman on the stoop vanished again behind the night into herself. As she jogged that final incline, she watched anxiously for the glow, the shadow, the face. She found them all still there. Suddenly, she veered toward the porch and stopped about two feet shy of the front steps.

The woman's eyes widened with surprise. Dressed in a gray T-shirt and blue shorts, she flicked the ashes of her cigarette stub and smiled. The effect practically knocked her over.

"Did you get tired?" the woman asked, elbows resting on her thighs.

She lied. "It's hot. Too hot."

The woman pointed to the step where she sat. "Why not sit down?" She shifted left to make room. "You just moved in?"

The head turned, auburn hair tossed to one side.
"A few weeks ago. Name's Jackie Scott. Yours?"
"Lori. Lori Martin."
"Well, Lori, I've got a question."
She gulped for air and managed a nervous smile.
"What's that?"
From the cement floor between them, Jackie
reached for a pack of cigarettes and bumped her arm.
Sweat turned into goose bumps.
"Why do you run?"
"Why do I run?" she repeated.
"Yes, why? I mean, do you like it or what?"
Jackie struck a match. Her hand stopped short of the
cigarette in a Susan Hayward-like pose, pausing for
an answer.
"Well, no. I don't really like it." It was true.
Sometimes the monotony made her want to scream.
Until Jackie started watching. Then, suddenly,
running was everything. It was hard to express the
real reason. Everything she'd done before two weeks
ago seemed trivial.
"Then why?" Jackie asked again.
Relentless, unbending. She liked her. "I'm on the
university track team."
"Ahhh, so you're a student."
"Graduate student at Temple University."
"And a jock, too."
She laughed nervously. "Do I fit the stereotype?"
Jackie grinned and got up, walking down the
steps to the curb. Once there, she extinguished her
cigarette and looked back. "No. That's why I like
watching you. Power and grace. It's a beautiful
combination."
Lori felt her cheeks flush. Looking down at her

sneakers, she loosened the laces. "Thanks. But I've fallen on my face a few times."

"Haven't we all."

The summer nights fell into a pleasant rhythm. Jackie sat out on the stoop, listened to a portable radio, and watched Lori run. Several times a week Jackie invited her to dinner. Cooking turned out to be Jackie's hobby. She simmered delicate sauces, broiled fish, sautéed and stir-fried vegetables, boiled pasta, basted ribs. It sure beat the university cafeteria.

They went to the movies, shopped, ran errands. Mostly, they laughed and talked. Politics, current events, social issues, hobbies. One thing they never discussed was their friendship. But that didn't stop the questions in Lori's mind. She wondered, were they just neighbors, friends? She felt naive, anxious, uncertain. But truth be told, at that point in time, being with Jackie was enough.

Occasionally, she found herself trying to decipher Jackie's moods. She noticed a sadness about her, a detachment she couldn't quite grasp. Sometimes her friend seemed evasive and withdrawn. Then, just as suddenly, she was giddy, inquisitive, playful.

One night, in the middle of dinner, the phone rang.

Jackie sighed, threw her napkin on the table, and answered it in a clipped, hurried tone.

"Yes? I can't talk to you now," she snapped, turning slightly away. "I'm having dinner with a friend. A friend, that's all. None of your business. No, I won't do that. Besides, everything's final. Look, I told you, I can't talk right now."

Jackie hung up the phone. Her hands were shaking, face rigid. "Sorry. I hate when people call at the dinner hour."

"You all right?"

"Actually, I've lost my appetite. Would it be okay if we called it a night?"

"Yes, of course."

The following evening, Jackie was still in a difficult mood. Brooding, uncommunicative. Lori struggled to make conversation with her. "Do you have family in the area?"

"No," came the staccato reply.

Jackie was staring straight ahead and past her, as though she were a piece of furniture that needed to be moved.

"Do you have any family at all, Jackie?" She waved her hand in front of the woman's face. "Hello? Anybody home?"

Jackie returned from her thoughts and smiled. "Of course I have family. They live in Milwaukee. Okay?"

"Then how'd you end up in Philly?"

Ignoring the question, Jackie got up and started cleaning the counter, washing dishes, putting leftovers away. While Jackie fidgeted in the kitchen, she went into the living room. Turning on the stereo, she rotated the dial until she found a local FM station that played soft, adult contemporary music.

"You like that stuff?"

Jackie stood next to her, the front of her T-shirt wet, hands still damp from her clean-up chores.

"Sure."

"No rock? Rap? New wave?"

"Nope. I like relaxing music."

With that, she took Jackie's hand and coaxed her into the middle of the room. Insides churning, she pulled the woman close to her, putting her hands on either side of Jackie's waist. Through the thin T-shirt, she could feel the warmth of Jackie's skin as it curved toward her hips. For the first few moments, the woman in front of her appeared uncomfortable. Then Jackie grinned, resting a hand on each of her shoulders. As they moved slowly to the music, their eyes locked.

"Do you slow dance with all your neighbors?" Jackie asked.

Lori shrugged. "Haven't had too many dance partners lately. There was a guy from school who asked me out a few times."

"Did you like him?"

"He was okay. But he danced like King Kong."

Jackie tossed her head back and laughed. "I've danced with a few of those types." She raised her eyebrows. "What if he'd danced like Fred Astaire? Would you've liked him any better?"

"No."

"Makes you wonder, doesn't it?"

"What?"

"How life manages to get so screwed up."

Almost lovingly, Jackie's hand brushed her cheek. At that moment, something inside Lori's head snapped out of synch. She'd been staring at Jackie's soft lips, concentrating hard on not doing anything stupid. And then, with the touch of Jackie's hand, all resolve crumbled. Slowly, she leaned forward and kissed Jackie's mouth. Jackie responded by deepening the kiss, hands clasped behind her head. Eyes closed, she could feel every curve of Jackie against her. While they kissed, Lori moved her hands underneath the woman's T-shirt. Nervously, she caressed Jackie's breasts, her thumbs running across nipples hard with excitement. When the kiss ended, they both stood there, silently dazed. For one fleeting, precious moment, she saw it in Jackie's eyes — the happiness, the willingness, the one-tenth-of-a-second forward motion to kiss her again. To more than just kiss her. Then it was gone. Jackie stepped back, eyes suddenly glassy with tears.

"This is a mistake," she said, almost whispering. "But that pretty much describes my whole life." As if in pain, Jackie clasped her arms around her chest. "You want to know why my family's in Milwaukee and I'm in Philadelphia?" she assailed her without warning. "I moved because I got married!"

Lori felt a blow to her stomach — as though all her emotions, including Jackie's, had exploded in unison, landing there in that acidic pit to slowly burn, to slowly disintegrate. Married? Her jaw stuck open at its hinges. Heart pounding. Head drowning with sunken hopes. Jackie must've noticed the shock, the confusion.

"Listen, Lori, I should've told you before. I just didn't want to get into it."

Her own voice sounded far away. "You, your husband . . . Are you . . . ?"

"Divorced. I signed the papers last week."

"Why didn't you tell me? I thought . . ."

"Thought what?" Jackie interrupted. Her face was lined with frustration. "What are you? All of twenty-four?" She started to pace, arms still clutched to her chest. "God, you're just a kid! What could I have been thinking?" She did a quick three-sixty, eyes searing. "Know how old I am?"

Now Lori was getting angry. "Does it matter?"

"Yes, it fucking matters! Thirty-eight. Married six years. Six years of hell." Abruptly, Jackie strode to the recliner and slumped into it. "You'd think I would've learned something by now. God!" Leaning forward, she held her head in her hands. "Look, what I'm trying to say is, I wouldn't know where to begin, and you wouldn't know how to comprehend."

The next morning Lori knocked on Jackie's door. No answer. Each night she ran, watching for her, eyes burning into the darkness for a glimpse of a shadow on the stoop. The soft glow of a cigarette.

She thought a lot about Jackie's pain. And in her heart she knew Jackie was right. How could she understand? She felt inadequate, too young to give advice. What did she know? What words could she say? She'd never been in love. Sure, she'd had encounters, like the one with Mary Warner — the first woman she'd ever "done it" with. It'd been three years ago, in the backseat of an Isuzu Rodeo.

She kept hitting her head against the wheel well. Mary was unbuttoning her blouse, kissing her hard. She had no idea what to do.

"Mary, what . . ."

As if reading her mind, Mary answered, "It's okay, honey. I'll take care of everything."

Before she knew it, her jeans were down around her ankles, bra thrown over the backseat. Mary's kisses were suddenly directed to her breasts, her nipples disappearing into the woman's mouth. A hand slipped between her thighs. She could feel her own wetness, Mary's strong kisses. And the hand that explored and stroked her expertly until she came in about ten seconds flat. Then Mary's tongue went to work and Lori came again — thighs aching for more. She wondered how she and Mary had managed to fall in love so quickly.

It wasn't long until she realized that sex and love didn't necessarily go together. Minutes after their encounter, Mary was smoking a cigarette and talking nonchalantly, like they'd just finished bargain-shopping at the nearest mall . . .

☆ ☆ ☆ ☆ ☆

Thanks to Mary Warner, she knew she'd never been in love — until now. What she felt for Jackie went far beyond the backseat of any Rodeo.

It was a Wednesday night — the first week of September and two weeks after she'd last seen Jackie — that her evenly paced strides faltered a few yards from the front porch. Jackie was sitting there in total darkness. Only the glimmer of the full moon exposed her hunched shadow. Lori approached warily, her throat choking with words that wouldn't come.

"I've missed you," Jackie said finally.

"I've missed you, too."

Drawing on her cigarette, Jackie exhaled slowly, gray smoke trailing into the blackness. "It scared me being with you. I wasn't ready."

"For what?"

"Trust. Love. Passion." She crossed her arms in front of her. "A passion I've never felt before."

She sat down next to her, the smell of Jackie's perfume sweetening the stale, night air. "I'm sorry. I wanted to comfort you, but I didn't know how."

"Not your fault. It was me."

Jackie lit another cigarette. The glow from the match light illuminated her face — brown eyes flaring warmly, then fading as her breath extinguished the flame.

"My ex-husband's an oncologist at Fox-Chase," she continued. "We lived in Jenkintown. Three-story colonial, two-car garage. Immaculate green lawn. In-ground pool." She smiled wryly. "We had the perfect life."

"Why don't I believe you?"

"Because you're smart — and sensitive. You know better. And so do I." She laughed sarcastically. "Christ, I had no idea what marriage was all about. My parents divorced when I was three. I'm sure I never even loved John."

"Why did you marry him?"

"He asked, and I thought, well, it's getting kind of late in the game. I'm thirty-two. Guess I better say yes. But the whole marriage never felt right." Jackie looked at her and shrugged. "He never felt right." Getting up, she walked toward the curb, her face a remarkable silhouette in the moonlight. "Then he started hitting me. I can't remember when it began or why. It always seemed like it was some insignificant thing. Dinner served late. Shirts not ironed quite right. The wrong brand of deodorant. I only remember thinking that I was to blame because I never loved him." Jackie's eyes registered surprise, as though her own story seemed dreamlike, even to herself.

"It wasn't your fault. He was the one who didn't know anything about love. About partnerships."

"Yes, that's true. But it took three trips to the hospital and almost being killed to convince me — not to mention the ongoing therapy." She scraped a small stone around the pavement with her foot. For the first time she looked almost timid. "So, there I was, damaged baggage thrown on a strange doorstep, licking my wounds and feeling sorry for myself. Until one night you came running by." Jackie looked skyward, hands raised in frustration. "And then, suddenly, I understood everything. Ridiculous, isn't it?"

"Not really. I felt the same way."

Jackie returned to the porch, propping her foot on the lower step. "I guess we're just two lost hearts of summer, you and I."

"I don't think we're lost anymore."

Leaning forward, Jackie took Lori's hand, squeezing it softly. "No, we're not. I think we finally found what we've been looking for."

Three's a Crowd

Barbara Johnson

It was 1975 — Halloween night at All Souls'
Unitarian Church in Washington, D.C. Thunderous
applause boomed through the cavernous church as
Meg Christian took her final bows. The women who
filled the building to its rafters were standing,
stamping their feet, and shouting. The very structure
shook to its core. It was Meg's last encore, and she
finally disappeared behind the stage. The lights came
on as the clapping died down, and a collective sigh

echoed through the chamber. The audience was sorry to see the evening end.

Kevyn glanced over at her friends, Casey and Mary. She could tell from Mary's angry gestures and frowning face that they were having a bad argument. Casey didn't appear to be doing much talking, and soon Mary stormed away. In response to Kevyn's upraised eyebrows, Casey sauntered over.

"Mary's mad because she overheard me talking to you about Belinda," Casey said with a shrug of her shoulders. "She doesn't like it when I compliment other women. But what does she expect when she ignores me as she's been doing all night?"

Kevyn looked over at the object of Mary's ire. She had to admit that Belinda looked particularly fetching tonight, dressed plainly in jeans and an embroidered Indian cotton blouse. It was the blouse that had prompted Casey's comments. Belinda's ash-blond hair, fashionably long and straight, swayed with every movement of her head, and her green eyes sparkled with animation. Kevyn was glad she'd been able to bring Belinda out that night for the concert. She and her lover attended different universities and lived at home with their respective parents while they worked to make enough money to move in together. It was hard to get away together, especially because the parents were hostile to Belinda's and her relationship. Kevyn returned her attention to Casey, who was lucky enough to have parents who were completely supportive.

"So, what are you gonna do?" Kevyn asked. "You going after her?"

Casey shook her head. "Nah. I told her she could go home with her buddies."

Kevyn was a bit surprised at Casey's indifference. "You sure?"

From the vantage of their balcony seats, Casey looked down at the throng of women below. "She's probably already on the way home."

At that moment, Belinda joined them. "Where's Mary?"

Casey answered. "We had a fight. I told her to go home."

Belinda raised her right eyebrow but said nothing.

"Well," Kevyn said, "how about going out for a bite to eat? Blimpie's in Georgetown? Should be lots of interesting Halloween action going on."

Casey and Belinda nodded, and the trio maneuvered their way down the stairs and into the main hall of the church. The place was still crowded with women, and the high energy and excitement from the concert seemed to electrify the room.

The three friends finally exited into the cool night air. The streets were busy. Lights from all the cars glowed like diamonds and rubies in the darkness. High overhead in a dark, cloudless sky, the full orange moon lent atmosphere to the spooky holiday. Casey quickly located her white VW bug. They paused on the sidewalk.

"You know, we'll have trouble finding parking in Georgetown," Casey stated. "Still want to go?"

Kevyn looked at Belinda's happy face. The little cafe whose specialty was submarine sandwiches was Belinda's favorite. "Sure," she answered.

They folded themselves into the VW and drove off. Kevyn wished she'd been able to borrow her mother's car that night. It was nice of Casey to drive — like she usually did, being the only one of the three with her own car — but if Kevyn had the car she could take Belinda home tonight and maybe steal a few hours in Belinda's bed before dawn. They'd done it before, sneaking into the house and down to the basement where Belinda had her bedroom. Her parents' room was directly overhead, and many a time Kevyn had to cover Belinda's mouth with her hand to stifle her moans. An hour or so before dawn, Kevyn would creep out of Belinda's house and drive back to her own. She liked to believe that they had both sets of parents fooled, but she doubted it.

It wasn't long before they were cruising around the residential streets of Georgetown looking for a parking space. They got lucky; a Mercedes pulled out not three blocks from Blimpie's. The three women piled out of the car and quickly headed for the cafe, passing several groups of people in various costumes and stages of intoxication.

Once inside Blimpie's, they ordered their sandwiches at the counter, watched the cute redhead make them, and then carried their trays to the back of the cafe. Belinda found herself sitting between Kevyn and Casey, a not unpleasant situation. The closeness of the two dark-haired women stirred feelings in her that she had only dared fantasize about. She glanced at Kevyn seated on her right. She was broad shouldered and amply endowed, with dark-brown hair that fell almost to her shoulders and laughing hazel eyes that crinkled when she smiled. Her strong arms and hands had driven Belinda to distraction on more than one occasion. She was much shorter than Belinda, a characteristic that Belinda didn't mind at all.

Kevyn and Casey were in animated conversation, discussing some upcoming sports event at the University of Maryland. Belinda bit delicately into her shrimp salad sandwich before letting her eyes wander over the woman sitting on her left. Casey was a bit shorter than Kevyn but just as broad shouldered. Her short hair, black as midnight, was thick and just made for running one's fingers through. The expression in Casey's dark eyes let a woman know exactly what she wanted.

Belinda squirmed a bit in her seat. She wondered what it would be like to make love with both women at once. It was an idea that had crossed her mind before. She felt the hot flush on her cheeks and guiltily closed her eyes. What could she be thinking? A *ménage à trois*? What would Kevyn think? What would Casey? She opened her eyes. The two women on either side seemed to be sitting nearer than ever.

"Well, well, well," Casey said in a low husky voice, "take a look at that."

Belinda and Kevyn followed her discreet finger. A stunning blonde in a black satin Playboy Bunny costume walked precariously on spike heels to the back of the cafe. A tall pirate accompanied her, but the three women paid him no mind. The blonde more than filled out her costume. As she slid around the table to sit down, the white puff of fur on her shapely ass seemed to tease and beckon.

"I wouldn't mind playing with that powder puff," Casey said with a twinkle in her eye. Her mouth turned up at one corner in a lecherous grin.

"You're not kidding," Kevyn replied with a glance at Belinda. She put her arm around her girlfriend's shoulders. "Why don't you wear one of those, honey?"

Belinda rolled her eyes. "You two are terrible. Are you done? Let's head home."

The three found Casey's VW and headed out of the city into the Virginia suburbs. They were animated on the drive home, talking about the concert and upcoming midterms and the latest happenings at the women's center. Belinda envied Casey and Kevyn; they attended the University of Maryland where such things as a women's center existed. She attended a Virginia university that had barely heard of feminism.

All too soon they arrived at Belinda's house. Casey pulled into the driveway and cut the engine. Belinda was relieved to see that no lights were on inside the house. That meant her parents hadn't waited up. In the backseat, Belinda curled her hand inside Kevyn's and laid her head on Kevyn's shoulder.

"I don't want you to go," she said softly. "I don't want the night to end."

Kevyn tilted Belinda's chin to kiss her softly on the mouth. "I know, sweetheart, but Casey has to work early tomorrow."

Belinda felt daring. She touched Casey lightly on the shoulder. "You know, my parents have a sofa bed in the basement where my bedroom is. You could spend the night, too. I promise I'd wake you up in time to go to work."

Casey was tempted, but she had to be at work at eight. She looked at her watch. That was only six hours away — if you didn't count the hour-long drive back to Maryland. She looked at Belinda's pleading green eyes, and her resolve melted. Casey knew that Kevyn and Belinda didn't have many opportunities to spend the night together. Who was she to stand in the way of true love?

"Oh, okay."

"You're a sweetheart," Belinda said as she leaned over the seat and kissed Casey on the cheek.

They got out of the car and walked quietly around to the back door of the house. Belinda unlocked the door as quietly as possible. She didn't want to wake her parents or siblings or dogs. No such luck. The dachshund and the fox terrier waited with wagging tails as she stepped into the kitchen. Belinda bent down to pet them.

"Shhhh. Go on to bed," she whispered as she pointed to the doorway leading out of the kitchen.

Obediently, the two dogs disappeared down the darkened hallway. Belinda motioned for Kevyn and Casey to follow her down the stairs to the basement. She breathed a sigh of relief as she turned on the light.

"I am so glad Mom and Dad weren't up," she said as she unfolded the sofa.

Kevyn bent to help her. "You and me both." She straightened and looked at Casey. "You're really lucky that your parents are so cool."

"That's what women tell me all the time," Casey replied with a grin. She flopped onto the bed. "Have fun, you two," she said with a knowing wink.

Belinda felt the blush warm her face. Kevyn pulled her quickly into the bedroom and closed the door, but not tightly. It was still the typical bedroom of a young girl — gold and white French provincial furniture, stuffed animals, posters on the pale green walls, clothes draped over the chair and on the floor. It was a familiar place to both Belinda and Kevyn, a place Kevyn secretly thought of as much too feminine.

They hurriedly pulled off their clothes in the dark and climbed into the double bed. The small basement window on the wall above the head of the bed filtered in light from the streetlamp. The two women snuggled together briefly before Kevyn pulled Belinda to her and kissed her deeply.

In the other room, Casey listened to the murmuring sounds of love and squirmed in her lonely bed. For a moment she regretted her fight with Mary. Would she have been allowed to have Mary in this bed? Most probably. Kevyn and Belinda took every opportunity to sleep together. Casey knew she and Kevyn would probably leave before dawn's light, to be sure that Belinda's parents didn't know what had gone on in their basement. She looked up at the ceiling. Just where *was* their room?

In the bedroom, Belinda momentarily stopped Kevyn's roving hands. Impulsively, she dared a suggestion. "Don't you think Casey is awfully lonely out there?"

Kevyn smiled and got out of bed without a word. She pulled on a T-shirt and went to the door and pushed it open. She could see Casey on the sofa bed. Was she already asleep?

Casey heard a sound and turned her head to the bedroom door. It was open now as Kevyn stood there in a T-shirt and motioned for her to come. Casey sat up. She pointed to the bedroom with a questioning glance. Kevyn smiled and nodded. *Hmmm. This could prove interesting,* Casey thought as she got out of bed and complied.

Kevyn quickly walked around the foot of the bed

and got into the right side. Casey, still wearing her
underwear and a T-shirt, slid under the covers on
the left. Belinda lay on her back between them.
Casey could tell immediately that Belinda was naked.
The very thought of Belinda's soft body made her
lick her lips. She had always thought that Belinda
was very pretty and sexy. She lay on her back and
let her hand rest ever so lightly against Belinda's
thigh.

Kevyn wondered what Casey was thinking. Did
she realize that Belinda was naked? Did she want to
make love to Belinda? Kevyn knew that Belinda had
thought about making love with Casey. At first it had
made her jealous, but now the idea of her and Casey
driving Belinda crazy with lust was very appealing.

Belinda was dealing with a stirring of emotions
that she had never felt before. She could feel her
rapid heartbeat, the butterflies in her stomach. She
concentrated on lying perfectly still and keeping her
breath even. She could feel Casey's hand softly
against her left thigh. Her fingers seemed to burn.
Belinda felt the fire spread across her skin and
between her legs.

As if on cue, Kevyn and Casey both rose up on
one elbow and stared silently down at the woman
lying between them. Belinda looked first at one, then
the other. She shrank a little into the pillow, but not
fearfully. Her dark-haired companions smiled and
then leaned down to kiss her. Two pairs of lips on
her neck; Belinda felt the rush of heat course
through her body. Kevyn's and Casey's hands slid
across her body and met briefly on her stomach. She
squirmed as their fingers edged lower, and lower still.
She moaned deeply as Casey kissed her full on the

mouth while Kevyn sucked a tender nipple into her mouth. Belinda arched her back and grabbed each woman.

Casey felt her own heart beat faster in response to Belinda's moan. She looked up briefly from her kiss to watch Kevyn descend on Belinda's nipple. She kissed Belinda's eager lips once more and then moved to her sensitive throat.

Kevyn changed tactics and slid from Belinda's breasts to her stomach and then lower still. Belinda's legs spread involuntarily. Kevyn dipped her fingers deep; Belinda was wet and so ready. She took Kevyn's fingers easily. Kevyn heard Belinda's indrawn breath as she touched her tongue to Belinda's clitoris. She felt Casey's hand on her head, pushing her down. Or was it Belinda's hand?

It seemed only seconds before Belinda felt the waves of orgasm. Her legs tensed as her senses exploded with the intense stimulation from all over her body. It was as if a hundred hands caressed her and just as many mouths kissed her and licked her and nipped her gently. And how many fingers penetrated her, pushed into her, reached far into tender places? Her moans were smothered by Casey's mouth. Or was it Kevyn's? She clutched the sheets, and then the strong shoulders of the woman between her legs. Her climax receded like a warm tide.

Belinda collapsed into the pillows. She took several deep breaths. The filtered light from the window only revealed shadowy forms that hovered above her. She couldn't tell who was who. But the two women weren't done with her.

Silently, Kevyn and Casey changed places. Casey's hand delved where Kevyn's had been only moments before; her mouth traced the same path that Kevyn's had taken. Kevyn kissed Belinda's tender, swollen lips. As she watched Casey's head dip lower, she fought back a twinge of jealousy and instead smothered Belinda's cry with her mouth.

Unbelievable as it seemed, Belinda felt the beginnings of a second orgasm. She grabbed the short hair of the woman between her legs and pushed into her mouth. She thrust her hips upward, taking Casey's fingers deeper still. The orgasm rippled across her body. The lips on her lips took her breath away, making her moan and yet stilling her moan at the same time. Exhausted, she felt her whole body go limp. Her exquisite torment was over.

Casey and Kevyn smiled into the darkness. They still said not one word. Casey moved up to rest beside Belinda. She lay on her left side, cradling her head in the crook of her elbow and placing her right hand gently on Belinda's belly. Kevyn nestled against Belinda and traced her fingers softly across Belinda's shoulders and down over her breasts until they too rested on Belinda's belly. Her hand touched Casey's. Their fingers intertwined. She smiled and closed her eyes as she felt her own body relax.

Across the bridge of Belinda's body, Casey smiled too.

King Louie

Jackie Calhoun

The first time ever . . .

When I fell in love with a long-necked sorrel gelding, I was trailing after my best friend, whom I'd pursued mutely for more than a year. Connie was searching for a horse suited for my meager talents. The prerequisite descriptors were *gentle, kind, well broken.* In other words, I needed an animal that would take care of me. Actually, I only wanted a horse because it would give me a good reason to frequent Connie's barn more often than I already did.

We stood in a fellow horse owner's large stable on a cool March day while he told us about King Louie. Louie gazed at us from the patient depths of large brown eyes. He neighed softly. Another horse called from the pasture, and he whinnied an answer. He had friends. *How often has he been sold?* I wondered. Connie had told me not to project human feelings onto horses, but I couldn't help it.

"He's from King stock," Ace Thompson said. "He's got sixty-five western pleasure points. Are you planning to show him?"

"Maybe," Connie said, smiling at me. "Leah needs a gentle, dependable ride."

I grinned back, my heart in my throat. Was showing Louie part of the high price I paid for being in love with a horse-minded woman?

"He's all of that and more. Want to try him?" Ace slid the stall door open and haltered Louie, who stood placidly waiting. He cross-tied the horse in the aisle and curried him down.

Connie grabbed a brush and helped. I stood nearby watching the dirt fly off Louie's coat. The smell of horses — dust, manure, grain, hay — filled my nostrils. I was close enough to sniff Louie's breath, fragrant and warm with the odor of sweet feed on it.

When Louie was saddled, Ace rode him in the enclosed riding arena to warm him up. Then he and Connie looked at me.

"You ride him first, Connie," I said, knowing she was dying to. I certainly wasn't.

She put the reins over Louie's neck and mounted easily. After straightening the saddle, she walked

Louie halfway around the arena before putting him
into a trot. He looked good. I knew the signs. His
head hung at a natural angle to his neck, which
poked out straight from his withers. His back was
flat; his hindquarters under him. His trot was
consistently slow and inherently graceful. Lifting the
reins a little, Connie asked for a lope. Louie correctly
picked up her lead and gave her a rocking-horse
canter. He appeared to be a comfortable ride.

And Connie looked wonderful — her body molded
to Louie's, her movements synchronized with his. I
had thought she was gorgeous from the beginning,
but when I first saw her on horseback, I wanted her.
My desire had become an ache that sharpened
whenever Connie rode and sent chills through my
groin and down my legs.

She dismounted and held the reins for me. Where-
as she vaulted into the saddle in one fluid motion, I
put my foot in the stirrup, hopped a few times with
the other foot, grabbed the pommel of the western
saddle, and hauled myself up. Once on top, I
surveyed the earth as a safe place.

Until Louie, I had never felt truly secure on a
horse. Louie waited patiently while I, too, settled the
saddle in its proper place. In an imitation of Connie I
took the reins, and the horse walked away with me. I
didn't have to ask Louie to hug the wall; he did it
naturally, and my body moved with the cadence of
his walk. At the far side of the pen I asked him for
a trot. Ace said a little squeeze was all it took. Louie
trotted off, making me look like a pro. I loved him
for it. A slight bump on the bit brought him down to
a walk. From there I signaled for a canter by picking

up the reins a tad and pressing my heel against his outer side. He lifted himself into a lope and rocked me around the ring. I didn't have to concentrate on his performance. All I had to do was sit deep in the saddle and not give him the wrong cues.

After passing Connie and Ace both ways at a canter, I shortened the reins a bit and whispered, "Whoa." Louie skidded to a stop, throwing me forward. Regaining my balance, I rode toward them with a grin on my face. I wanted Louie. A horse that could make me look like I was in command was hard to find.

"What's your bottom price?" Connie asked Ace.

Toeing the dark arena dirt with his boot, Ace aimed a stream of snuff off to the side. "The owners want eighty-five hundred for him. I'll be glad to take your offer to them."

That was way over my limit. I had five thousand to spend.

"Well, he's eleven hears old," Connie said with a glance at me. I knew my disappointment showed. "Would they consider five?"

"He's got all those pleasure points." He shrugged and spit again. "Don't hurt to ask, though."

Connie's F-350 supercab bolted down the road toward her place. "Even pulling a trailer full of horses, this truck is a runaway." She grinned at me, making my heart pound with joy. "How'd you like Louie?"

"I loved him." I should be so lucky to own such a horse. My last horse and the one before it had been mean-spirited, headstrong animals who had either run off with me or refused to leave the barn.

"You looked good on him. Good enough to show. Can you swing any more than five thousand?"

"I don't think so." The bank had promised to add that amount onto my car loan. I'd be in hock for five years. I gave King Louie up in my mind. I wasn't meant to have him.

I hung around the barn and helped Connie with the chores — cleaning stalls, feeding and watering, filling stock tanks in the two pastures.

Connie was a knockout in blue jeans. She was tall and slender with cinnamon-colored hair that fell to her shoulders in a loose perm and blue-black eyes fringed by curling lashes. Her fearlessness captured my imagination. I thought maybe it would rub off on me. She was at ease when handling a horse or riding one.

When we went inside the house, I was cold. She lit the kindling in the fireplace and put water on the stove. We sat in front of the fire, feeding logs to it until it took hold. Then Connie closed the glass doors.

The kettle whistled, and I went to the kitchen to fill a couple of mugs with boiling water and chocolate. We leaned on our elbows, our feet stretched toward the flames. For the first time that day, I began to heat up. I shivered as the chill left me.

"You okay, Leah?" she asked, looking momentarily concerned.

I nodded, thinking about her. Her parents owned the little house she lived in and the barn and acreage that surrounded it. They paid her to take care of the horses, to show them. She took young, inexperienced animals with potential — the ones who possessed and moved with that indefinable look of class — and put points on them in the quarter horse shows. Then she sold them, sometimes for ten times what she'd paid.

"I could buy him, you could show him," she said, her face rosy in the firelight.

"I thought he had to be in my name for me to show him amateur." The offer warmed me. It gave me hope. Perhaps she cared as much about me as I did her.

"He does. I could loan you the money."

I smiled at her. "Thanks. It's always a mistake to lend friends money."

"Let's see what Ace comes up with. Maybe you'll get him for five." She drank from her mug. "Spend the night, why don't you?"

I'd stayed last weekend. It was torture to sleep in her bed, though, and there was just the one bedroom. The other she used as an office. Still, I knew I would stay whenever she asked. "Thanks."

Against my better judgment, I let her purchase Louie. I agreed to buy him from her in monthly installments. To get around the American Quarter Horse rules for amateurs, King Louie was registered with me as the owner. It wasn't kosher, but it was the only way I'd ever own a piece of Louie.

As temperatures rose, I worked frantically to be ready for the spring shows. Connie was already showing, of course. She'd gone to the Gold Coast and some of the other early circuits. When she was gone, I took care of the horses left behind. She had a four-year-old gelding who was more often than not in the winnings. But it wasn't the show money she was after, although that paid her expenses. It was the quarter horse points.

She drove in from a show one Sunday night in May while I was in the barn, feeding. My pulse hammered when the horses whinnied an answer to her gelding. Unloading him, she put him in his stall. She'd won the junior and amateur pleasure classes, she told me in answer to my questions.

"You must be tired," I said, soaking up the sight of her. "I can grill something for supper if you want." I'd spent the weekend at her place and had stocked the refrigerator with food.

"That's an offer I can't refuse." Filling the gelding's water bucket, she went to fetch him grain and hay.

She showered while I made hamburger patties, heated up leftover baked beans in the microwave, and pulled out chilled pasta salad. I was none too clean myself, having spent the afternoon with the horses, and when she emerged with wet hair tangled down her back, I jumped in for a quick wash.

After I got out of the shower, I leaned into the mirror. Short, black hair covered my head with disorderly curls. In the sunburst of my face, my hazel eyes looked very dark. I felt the heat radiating from my skin. I'd forgotten to use suntan lotion.

We ate on the screened-in porch as evening fell over the acreage and gradually obscured the fields until only the barn was lit by the dusk-to-dawn light.

The soft breeze reminded me that summer was nearly there. Moths and early June bugs battered themselves in futile efforts to get to the candles lighting the card table where we sat.

I thought about what I wanted to say to her, how to phrase it. There would never be a better time. "I like you too much," I murmured, nearly choking on the words.

She let a few moments go by, while I squirmed over my admission, before saying softly, "So do I."

I stayed that night. But I didn't have the nerve to reach for her, nor did she make a move in my direction. Instead, I squeezed my eyes shut, hoping in vain that sleep would sneak up on me. I heard her deep and even breathing.

We went to a nearby open show the following Friday evening, where I entered the same western classes that Connie did. She took a three-year-old whom she'd just started to show. I was so nervous that I made four trips to the john before my first class.

Connie put several horses between us when she entered the show pen. She didn't want her young horse trying to keep up with Louie. I kept my eyes on where I was going, one hand on the reins, one by my side, heels down, sitting deep in the saddle. I was tired from all the preparations that go into show-ing — clipping and bathing horses, cleaning tack, getting clothes ready, loading the trailer. Why Connie thought this was so much fun was beyond me. Maybe she didn't think about it that way since it was her profession, so to speak.

We went through our paces — walk, trot, lope on the rail in both directions. For the untrained eye, it looked like a tiresome business. But to be performing in front of others wasn't a bit boring. It was a joy to be on a horse who knew how to win a pleasure class.

I looked across the arena once and saw Connie's three-year-old acting up. She had both hands on the reins, training him. She went to open shows, so that she could ready a young horse for the quarter horse shows.

The judge motioned some horses off the rail, starting with Louie. That could mean we'd won first place or sixth or maybe we'd just made the cut. But we were among the finalists, I knew that much from watching those still riding — Connie included.

Connie was excused from the ring along with the others who weren't going to place. She positioned herself where I'd pass near the gate. When the judge put the rest of us back on the rail, she offered me encouragement as I trotted by. "Doing great. Keep it up. Looking good."

When I next floated past her, it was at a lope. I heard her say, "Good show. You're gonna win this one."

I did too. Ace was the announcer. He called my name and King Louie's, saying, "I sold her that horse, ladies and gentlemen. She done good. Give her a hand." Clapping accompanied Connie's whistles and shouts.

When I left the arena with my envelope of uncounted winnings, Connie pulled me off Louie. She danced me around, kissing and hugging me.

We went to bed that night clad only in bikini panties and undershirts. The dusk-to-dawn light cast the shadow of a beech tree across the bedroom floor and against the walls.

"You like winning?" Connie asked, resting on an elbow, looking down at me. Her sun-bleached hair covered her shoulder, and I resisted the urge to brush it back.

My heart pounded at the sight of her teasing smile. "It could easily become addictive," I said truthfully. It probably already was for her. No wonder she didn't mind the work that went into showing.

"I had fun tonight, having you along."

"You drive me crazy," I whispered, surprising myself. Where had that come from? I held my breath, staring at her shadowed eyes, waiting for a reply.

"Do I?" She straddled me as if I were a horse, her gaze still caught by mine. Slowly, she stretched out on top of me, her hair raining down around my face. When we kissed, her breath tasted sweet.

I stopped breathing for a moment, and my heart leapt around my chest like a wild thing. I saw that her eyes had closed. But I wanted to record every detail of this first time: the soft lips, the touch of tongue, the sure hands on my skin, the supple body pressed against mine.

Come on, I told myself. *Make a move. Don't lie here like a lump.* Putting my arms around her, I began a hesitant caress. Her skin was warm and slightly sweaty.

Raising herself, she pulled her undershirt upward to uncover her breasts. Then she did the same with mine, watching the unveiling. After, she lowered herself onto me once more and closed her eyes. A little moan escaped her.

I could have kissed her forever, never going any further. She made the moves, wrapping her legs around one of mine, sliding a hand down the length of me. When she cupped my breast, taking my nipple in her mouth, I felt the tugging in my groin. Her hand continued over my rib cage, my hip, my thigh. With agonizing slowness, her palm slid up the inside of my upper leg and covered my crotch. I moved against it.

"Let's take these clothes off," she whispered in my ear. The unexpected sound startled me. Lifting herself to her knees she removed her undershirt and panties, then helped me out of mine.

I had seen her naked, of course, but had never felt free to look. Her skin glowed, her breasts sloping outward toward the darker nipples, then making a full curve in toward her ribcage. On her knees like that, I could count her ribs and see her hip bones framing her flat belly. The dark pubic hair shadowed the space between her slender thighs.

She settled next to me, drawing me tightly against her, so that I felt the softness of our breasts. I sighed as we resumed kissing, reaching deeper with our tongues. Her hand moved down my spine to my hips and around to the joining of my legs. I lifted a thigh to let her in. Taut with expectation, I waited for her fingers to find me.

The muscles beneath her smooth skin moved under my touch. Her back was long, her buttocks small and tight. I, too, slid my hand over her hip and into her crotch. Feeling my way through the dense curls, I was emboldened by her quick breathing.

We lay face to face, holding each other close, lips and breasts pressed together, each bending a leg upward, our fingers caressing. The long, slow strokes drew from me a deep pleasure that I couldn't contain. I felt myself moving, heard myself moaning. I curbed my passion only by concentrating on her.

When she pulled away from me and rose once more to her knees, I groaned a protest. She kissed my lips, took my breasts to suckle, brushed my belly with her lips and, turning head to toe, went down on me. I froze, but when she spread my legs and touched me with her tongue, her fingers slowly working their way inside, I lost the last measure of control.

Wrapping my arms around her hips, I drew her down to taste her. Gratified, I heard her moans grow louder, felt her body convulse.

Struggling for breath, I waited for the pounding of my heart to subside.

Rolling off me, she turned around and took me in her arms. When she spoke, her voice was hoarse. "Am I as exciting as Louie?" She kissed my ear, my lips.

I kissed her back. "You're each thrilling in your own way."

Laughing, she hugged me close. "He's tough competition. I should feel flattered."

The smell of sex excited me anew. "How about another round?"

"Later," she promised.

I whispered the fierce love I harbored for her.

"Me too," she murmured, slipping away from me into sleep.

Lying awake, staring at the shadows, running my fingers through her hair, I savored contentment.

Rising to the Bait

Dorothy Tell

I fidgeted against the vinyl seatback of a booth in the Liar's Grill as I waited for my fishing partner to arrive. V.J.'d said not to worry, she'd find me. Okay, I told myself. *Finding* me is not the worry, is it? I couldn't quite bring myself to name the real worry.

I thought I knew my own mind, but apparently I didn't. I was doing things I hadn't done in decades — turning in front of the mirror to see what my rear looked like in my new jeans or, rather, to see if it looked anywhere near good. If menopause hadn't

reminded me I still had body parts below the waist, I
think I might've forgotten altogether.

But based on the warmth between my legs at this
moment, I must admit my attention had been got.
How could I have let this happen?

From the first time I met V.J. at my widow's
support group, I was drawn to her strength of
personality, to her almost chivalrous manner towards
the rest of the women in the group. Of course she
made it perfectly clear right up front about her
lesbianism, and I thought it very courageous of her.
Her stoic grieving was certainly as real as anyone's.
More so than some, I suppose — me, for instance.
The long shut-in years of caring for Ben after his
stroke had drained me of feeling. I was more relieved
than anything when his heart finally gave out. But
the sudden loneliness I felt was as dark as any
despair I'd ever known. The more I became aware of
the world around me, the more I felt the need for
someone to share it with.

I looked up to find V.J. striding toward my table
in her usual energetic manner, short graying curls
still holding the shape of the baseball hat she rolled
and stuffed into her jacket pocket. Her blue eyes
reflected the unclouded vistas of the water and sky of
her beloved outdoors.

She smiled as she slid into the booth across from
me. "Ready to go, Rookie? All you need is your
fishing license. You got that, right?"

I nodded, reluctantly unclasping my cold fingers
from the warm coffee cup. Filled with equal parts of
excitement and hesitation, I allowed myself to be led
from the noisy comfort of the Liar's Grill into the
sparkling morning.

I climbed into the cab of my new friend's red pickup truck and watched in the rearview mirror as she did a walk-around of the matching boat and trailer. Her long legs were slim and muscular, and when she stretched up to adjust a tie-down, I could see that her narrow waist gave way to nice hips. Some part of me was still concerned that I'd chosen the only lesbian in my widow's support group to be my friend. I told myself that my sexual reawakening had nothing at all to do with V.J. herself; it was just a natural phase in recovering my zest for living... and, of course, V.J. and I'd had long and frank discussions about what our "issues and boundaries" were.

I wanted a friend, and so did she. I needed to renew my soul and become reacquainted with the outdoors after the long suffocating years of Ben's illness. And V.J. needed a fishing partner, someone to laugh at her offbeat jokes. And heaven knew *I* needed something to smile at.

The pickup ride was brief, and my consciousness seemed filled by an acute awareness of V.J.'s physical presence on the seat beside me as she drove and told me stories of her childhood as the only daughter born to a farming family who already had eight sons.

Within the narrow space of half an hour, we were on the water in the shiny red bass-boat headed for one of V.J.'s favorite fishing spots, and my thoughts turned to the beauty of the water. The lake surface was furrowed with rows of rolling waves, and when we turned into the wind the boat lifted and sliced cleanly through each crest. Nothing in my experience had prepared me for the wild exhilaration of this dash across the water. The roar of the powerful

outboard engine made conversation impossible, and I
let myself sink into the protecting cocoon of sound
and sun and spray and the hypnotic thump of the
hull against the waves.

I watched V.J. with appreciation as she deftly
navigated the craft away from the open water and
under the arched span of a low highway bridge that
opened into a calm cove where the surface was
broken only by the standing trunks of dead trees.
The dark, green shoreline glimmered in the near
distance, slashed occasionally where craggy rocks
spilled across narrow points of land.

V.J. cut the engine and tied up to the bridge
abutment. In the deep silence my senses were all
magnified. The sun's warmth soaked into my body,
and my hearing picked up even the tiniest sounds of
bubbles bursting on the face of the clear green water.
My nose registered the pungent odors of aquatic
growth and decay, and my gaze was everywhere at
once. The blueness of the sky against the lush greens
of the treetops, the neon pink and staccato design of
V.J.'s jacket danced against my eyelids. I felt my
chest swell, and something long-buried moved through
my heart and crept into my arms and legs. I had
been so long devoid of happiness that it took the
sound of V.J.'s voice to make me understand my
feelings were showing.

"Whatcha grinning at, Marge?"

To my dismay, I felt my throat close, and I
blinked against the sudden sting of tears as I tried to
answer. Not since my first week of hormone replace-
ment had I experienced such an abrupt emotional
shift. Concern sobered V.J.'s face as she climbed over
the livewell and sat across from me. She removed her

sunglasses and slid them in her pocket with a smooth, one-handed flip, then took my hands in hers and bent toward me, peering intently into my eyes. "Are you okay?"

"Yeah." I swallowed around the lump in my throat and tried not to notice the warmth of V.J.'s hands. "I think I'm just *happy* for the first time in years, if that makes any sense to you."

V.J. let go of my hands and offered me a Kleenex from her pocket. I saw the tiny muscles around her eyes reflect painful memories of her own loss, and I wanted to take back my words. She turned her head, but not before I caught the glint of tears.

"It makes a *lot* of sense . . ." She began, then cleared her throat and took off her hat, turning it so the bill was in front. She jammed it back on her head, adjusting it to hide her eyes. "I'm hoping for happy myself one of these days." Then her face softened and she smiled. "You ready for your fishing lesson?"

I nodded, pleased to see she wasn't going to let my thoughtless words get in the way of what we'd come to do. I watched and listened as she explained all the various equipment and methods for catching a black bass. I hadn't expected fishing to be so specialized. Before today I'd thought one fish much like another, but V.J. set me straight on that account. Oh no, the type of bait and the way it was presented was most important if one wanted to catch a specific fish.

"See," she said, as she handed me a rod and reel and picked up her own. "What we're doing today is called 'flipping' for bass. You don't cast the plastic worm way out over the water; you just pull a little line out with your free hand and let it go as you flip the end of the rod." She leaned forward, demonstrating what she meant for me to do.

Though I was unaccountably aware of the way V.J.'s T-shirt clung to her breasts as she manipulated the rod tip, I managed to follow her example and watched as the bubblegum-pink *Sluggo* attached to my hook sank into the shimmering darkness alongside a weathered tree trunk. I almost dropped the rod when the water boiled up and the tree quivered as a fish of enormous size leaped into the air, twisting its broad body as it tried to rid its mouth of the hook V.J. had hidden in the soft plastic lure.

V.J. let out a whoop and stationed herself behind me. "Quick — set the hook! Here, girl — let me help you." She reached around, placing her hands over mine on the rod handle. I felt her welcome strength calm the wobblies that'd reached my knees and elbows. The fish broke the surface again, flashing droplets of water into the sunshine.

"Hold her steady . . . now start to reel her in."

Somehow I managed not to lose my grip on the rod handle as I freed my left hand and wound the reel, winching the fighting bass closer to the boat. I felt V.J. reach away, then saw her left hand reappear holding a net. She leaned in close to me, fitting herself to my back and legs so we worked almost as one body, leaning back to lift the rod tip and swing the fish close to the net, then down as she brought the net around our prize.

In one motion we brought the fish into the boat and, beyond the thudding of my heart, I was acutely aware of two things. That the air was inordinately cool against my backside — and that a pulsing warmth had begun in a corresponding place on my front side.

Weak-kneed, I sat and watched V.J. as she unhooked the fish and stored it in the livewell. She shucked off her jacket, and the sun marked the firm muscles in her tanned arms and shoulders. She wore only a sleeveless T-shirt that hugged her torso, leaving no doubt about the pleasing shape of her bra-less bosom. She glanced up and caught me looking. I felt my face heat up.

She grinned and pushed her sunglasses up to ride atop her head. "Why, Marge, all this excitement has you flushed as a schoolgirl." Her eyes said something more. I tried to read exactly what, but she turned away and busied herself with straightening out my line and rehooking the *Sluggo*.

She was right. I was excited. Catching the fish was fun, but it had nothing to do with the largest part of what I was feeling. Suddenly I could think of nothing except what it would be like to feel V.J.'s arms around me again, to feel her mouth on mine. As the image grew in my mind, an electric giddiness gathered behind my knees and ran up my legs. It flashed through my body and squeezed the air from my lungs. I drew a ragged breath and tried to calm my runaway heartbeat.

V.J. stopped fussing with the fishing line and turned to face me. "Well, Marge . . " Her blue eyes sparkled and her level gaze probed deeply. "Did you like that?"

Now I knew what her eyes had meant. She knew I liked it. And she wasn't talking about catching the fish. She knew exactly what I was feeling, and that fact was playing hell with the amount of oxygen going to my brain.

Unable to trust my voice, I nodded. I felt my face and neck light up with a hot blush and was grateful when V.J. stopped looking at me so intently. She picked up a rod and trailed a lure in the water as she walked to the rear of the boat out of view behind me.

I felt the boat swing toward the bridge and realized V.J. had pulled the slack from our tether until we were back in the shadowy cavern of the arch. I felt her hands on my shoulders and her legs against my back. She knelt slowly, her body sliding down and setting me on fire everywhere we touched.

She turned me to face her. On her knees before me, she held me to her in a firm but tender embrace. My heart rocketed inside my chest with an energy long forgot. She edged closer to me, gently pressing my knees apart until I could feel her bosom beneath mine and her upturned face against my neck. Her mouth moved softly over my cheeks, and her breath came against my skin in short, hot puffs.

There weren't any words to say. None needed. None said. She pulled back from me, looking deeply into my eyes. What she saw must have answered any lingering doubt because she placed cushions beneath us, and then pulled me down until the firm, hot length of her lay against me — and then she kissed me.

Passion exploded in me. As my tongue answered hers, she began to touch all the places that shrieked for attention. Her strong hands were all over me. My

bra came loose, and her hot mouth covered my
nipple, building in me such craving desire that I felt
the first tightening of orgasm even before her hand
found my center.

She moaned as her fingers slipped easily into my
warm wetness. She stroked me firmly, circling my
raised clitoris and flicking it gently each time she
entered me. I had no time to feel the cool air against
my bare skin. Some part of my brain was trying to
make me notice where I was — in an open boat,
under a bridge, with my clothes in disarray while
another woman's hands and mouth on my body
brought me to a height of passion I'd never known.

I cried out as orgasm claimed me. The boat
rocked and bumped against the bridge; water slapped
against the hull; but nothing mattered except the
spewing volcano between my legs. V.J. lowered her
mouth and claimed me like no one had ever done
before. She owned me with her tongue. She kissed
me there until my body leaped like the fish —
twisting and turning, caught on the hook of her
tongue, drained of all except a growing need to give
what I had gotten.

V.J. finally released me and pulled away. She
removed her T-shirt in one fluid motion, then opened
her jeans and placed my hand against her pubic
mound. She kissed me, and the taste of my own body
on her lips produced in me such a visceral thrill that
whatever reticence I may have had left in a rush.

She closed her legs over my hand, holding my
fingers against her center, thrusting herself against
them only a few times before she stiffened and I
knew her release was coming. I moved my free hand

over her bare breasts, feeling the rich heavy warmth of each one as she moved, knowing — feeling — I had come home at last.

V.J. relaxed against me, sighing. She finally spoke, hesitant, it seemed, to break the magic of the moment. "I hope you understand, Marge, that what we just did means a lot more to me than fun in a boat."

A chuckle began somewhere under my ribs, and the sensation was as powerful and freeing in its own way as orgasm had been. *Happy* was good. I nodded, still not trusting my voice. I hadn't known I was going to *do* anything, but I was sure glad to hear it was special to V.J. Because now that I *had* done it, I wasn't about to *quit* doing it.

About the Authors

JACKIE CALHOUN is the author of *Lifestyles, Second Chance, Sticks and Stones, Friends and Lovers, Triple Exposure* and *Changes* (1995). She has published stories in *The Erotic Naiad* and *The Romantic Naiad*. Having recently finished her seventh book, she's beginning work on her eighth. She lives in Wisconsin with her significant other.

KATHLEEN COLLINS, born in the state of Washington in 1931, now lives near the shore of Long Island Sound. Retired from teaching, she writes, swims and walks the beaches, entertains friends, her grown children and young grandchildren. She has found local groups with whom to fight against hate mongers. Her last Naiad novel is *Lovers in the Present Afternoon.*

CATHERINE ENNIS and her lover of over twenty years live in a rural area of southern Louisiana. Catherine is the mechanic for her Model A Ford coupe, a gourmet cook, a gardener and runs a small business. Writing is an enjoyable hobby. This is her third short story.

LISA HADDOCK was born and raised in Tulsa, Oklahoma. She holds bachelor's and master's degrees from the University of Tulsa. Her other published works include the Carmen Ramirez mysteries *Edited Out* and *Final Cut.* A journalist working in New Jersey, she lives with her life partner and cats.

MELISSA HARTMAN teaches Creative Writing and English Literature to glassy-eyed skateboarders at Moorpark College in Southern California. Her novel, *The Sure Thing,* a romance between a seismologist who predicts earthquakes and a TV reporter caught in the flashpoint of the L.A. riots, was published by Naiad Press in 1994. The University of Southern California and the University of Nevada, Las Vegas, have published her poetry in their literary journals. She holds a master's degree in professional writing from U.S.C., completed her undergraduate work at

U.C.L.A., and has absolutely no interest in collegiate football. Now living in the Los Angeles area with Lyn Woodward, her lover of twelve years, Melissa grew up in New York City, where she started writing at the age of thirteen to impress her English teacher.

PENNY HAYES was born in Johnson City, New York, February 1940. As a child she lived on a farm near Binghamton, New York. She later attended college in Utica, Buffalo and Huntington, WV graduating with degrees in art, elementary and special education. She has made her living teaching in both New York State and in southern West Virginia. She presently resides in mid-state New York.

Ms. Hayes' interests include backpacking, mountain climbing, canoeing, traveling, reading, gardening and building small barns. She recently moved from living in a mobile home for the past fifteen years to a house on a foundation which she describes as finally coming home. When asked what she would do with fifteen hundred square feet in lieu of the seven hundred, eighty she had occupied for so long, grinning widely she replied without hesitation, "Rattle around."

Last summer she toured several New England states giving readings and talks regarding *Kathleen O'Donald.*

She has been published in *I Know You Know, Of the Summits and of the Forests* and various backpacking magazines. Her novels include *The Long Trail, Yellowthroat, Montana Feathers, Grassy Flats* and *Kathleen O'Donald.* She is currently working on her sixth novel set in the 1800s entitled *Now and Then.*

PEGGY J. HERRING lives in South Texas with her lover of nineteen years. A very rewarding stint in the Army from 1974–1977 deemed her fluent in Morse code for a short period of time. She and her partner, Frankie Jones, have been active in the lesbian community on local, state and national levels for several years. They currently serve on the state board for the Texas Lesbian Conference. Peggy truly believes that the only thing harder than writing a biographical sketch is answering the question, "And what is your book about?"

BARBARA JOHNSON is the author of *Stonehurst,* and her story "The Abbey" is included in *The Mysterious Naiad.* She is working on her third novel, *Valentine Moon.* Her novel *A Beach Affair,* was published by Naiad Press in August 1995.

Barbara still thinks about that Halloween night so long ago. The names in "Three's a Crowd" have been changed to protect the not so innocent.

SUSAN JOHNSON is the author of *Staying Power: Long Term Lesbian Couples* (Naiad Press, 1990), *When Women Played Hardball* (Seal Press, 1994) and *For Love and for Life* (Naiad Press, 1995), a collection of intimate profiles of lesbian couples who have been together ten years or more. In 1996 Naiad Press will publish her book *Lesbian Sex: An Oral History.* Everyone expects it to be extremely popular.

Susan is fifty-five years old, a writer and sociologist who lives in Anchorage, Alaska in her very own long term couple. Getting to her present state of bliss was, of course, itself a journey. And it all began with the first time ever.

KARIN KALLMAKER was born in 1960 and raised by loving, middle-class parents. From a normal childhood and equally unremarkable public school adolescence, she went on to obtain an ordinary Bachelor's degree from the California State University at Sacramento. At the age of sixteen, eyes wide open, she fell into the arms of her first and only sweetheart. Ten years later, after seeing the film *Desert Hearts,* her sweetheart descended on the Berkeley Public Library determined to find some of "those" books. "Rule, Jane" led to "Lesbianism—Fiction" and then on to book after self-affirming book by and about lesbians. These books were the encouragement Karin needed to forget the so-called "mainstream" and spin her first romance for lesbians. That manuscript became her first Naiad Press book, *In Every Port.* She now lives in Oakland with that very same sweetheart; she is a one-woman woman. Their family of two is soon to become three as they await the birth of their first child.

In addition to *In Every Port,* she has authored the best-selling *Touchwood, Paperback Romance, Car Pool* and *Painted Moon.* In 1996, look for *Wild Things* and after that *Embrace in Motion.* Since Karin considers her lesbian readers to be the only mainstream, she intends to write many more.

CLAIRE McNAB is the author of seven Detective Inspector Carol Ashton mysteries: *Lessons in Murder, Fatal Reunion, Death Down Under, Cop Out, Dead Certain, Body Guard* and *Double Bluff*. She has also written two romances, *Under the Southern Cross* and *Silent Heart*. While a high school English teacher in Sydney she began her writing career with comedy plays and textbooks. In her native Australia she is known for her self-help and children's books.

For reasons of the heart, Claire is now a permanent resident of the United States, although she tries to visit Australia at least once a year and warmly recommends her country as a breathtaking vacation destination.

ELISABETH NONAS has written three novels, *For Keeps* (1985), *A Room Full of Women* (1990), and *Staying Home* (1994), all published by Naiad Press. Her essay "Neighbors" is included in the anthology *Sister and Brother: Lesbians and Gay Men Write About Their Lives Together,* edited by Joan Nestle and John Preston (Harper San Francisco, 1994). She wrote the screenplay adaptation of Paul Monette's novel *Afterlife*. She has also published articles and short stories, and is the co-author with Simon LeVay of *City of Friends: A Portrait of Lesbian and Gay Culture* (MIT Press, 1995).

Elisabeth has taught fiction writing at the Institute of Gay and Lesbian Education in West Hollywood and at UCLA Extension, where she developed and taught the first lesbian and gay fiction writing classes offered there.

She is currently working on her fourth novel, *Promise Me*.

DIANE SALVATORE is the author of three novels — *Benediction, Love, Zena Beth,* and *Paxton Court* — and one collection, *Not Telling Mother: Stories From a Life.* She is also included in the anthology *The Romantic Naiad.* She is an editor at a national women's magazine, and lives in New Jersey with her partner of thirteen years, and their cocker spaniel.

CAROL SCHMIDT says that the first half of "Hippie Honeymoon" happened just that way, though in real life the incident had a boring ending: her husband came back and it took seven more years for her to finally come out. She is on the road full-time again, this time in a comfortable fifth wheeler RV with Norma Hair, her lover of sixteen years, plus a Shih Tzu dog and three cats. Their traveling household stops for all RVing Women rallies. Schmidt is the author of three novels of suspense published by Naiad — *Silverlake Heat, Sweet Cherry Wine,* and *Cabin Fever.*

ROBBI SOMMERS is the author of the best-selling books of erotica: *Pleasures, Players, Kiss and Tell, Uncertain Companions, Behind Closed Doors, Personal Ads* and *Getting There* — all published by Naiad Press. Born in 1950, she is the mother of three sons and a dental hygienist. In regards to "Backseat Driver" — although known to occasionally take the wheel . . . she prefers to be driven.

TERESA (T.) STORES is the author of *Getting to the Point* (Naiad Press, 1995). Her second novel, *Side Tracks,* the gender-fuck story of two Depression-era hobos — girls disguised as boys — who become lovers, is due to be published in June of 1996. Ms. Stores lives with two dogs, two cats, and a cute redhead in a small apartment in the New York area. She currently pays her bills by working as an editor (wearing a man's suit and tie) in conservative, corporate America. (Job offers welcome.)

DOROTHY TELL and her partner Ruth live in Texas where they look forward to the blessed event of Dot's retirement from the jobfromhell. They are shopping for a travel trailer and plan to hit the road for a while — a few months anyway — before they settle down to full-time writing. Between them, Dot and Ruth have three children, three grandchildren, assorted aging parents and twenty-three years of loving herstory. Dot's hobbies are woodcarving, knitting, fishing, shooting sporting clays and stretching canvases for Ruth's portraits and still lifes.

PAT WELCH was born in 1957 in Japan. She grew up in small towns in the south and relocated to California to attend college in Los Angeles. After moving to the San Francisco Bay area in 1986, she began the Helen Black mystery series for Naiad Press. Her most recent novel, *Open House,* is the fourth in the series. Pat also has a short story featured in *The Mysterious Naiad.* She lives and works in Oakland, California.

LAURA DeHART YOUNG has been a writer and editor of business publications for the past ten years. Her first novel, *There Will Be No Goodbyes,* was published by Naiad in April of 1995. Her second novel, *Family Secrets,* will be published by Naiad in 1996. She resides in Reading, Pennsylvania with her partner of eight years, two dogs and three cats.

A few of the publications of
THE NAIAD PRESS, INC.
P.O. Box 10543 • Tallahassee, Florida 32302
Phone (850) 539-5965
Toll-Free Order Number: 1-800-533-1973
Mail orders welcome. Please include 15% postage.
Write or call for our free catalog which also features an
incredible selection of lesbian videos.

PHASES OF THE MOON by Julia Watts. 192 pp. . . . . hungry
for everything life has to offer.   ISBN 1-56280-176-7 $11.95

BABY IT'S COLD by Jaye Maiman. 256 pp. 5th Robin Miller
mystery.   ISBN 1-56280-156-2   10.95

CLASS REUNION by Linda Hill. 176 pp. The girl from her past . . .
                                                 ISBN 1-56280-178-3   11.95

DREAM LOVER by Lyn Denison. 224 pp. A soft, sensuous,
romantic fantasy.   ISBN 1-56280-173-1   11.95

FORTY LOVE by Diana Simmonds. 288 pp. Joyous, heart-
warming romance.   ISBN 1-56280-171-6   11.95

IN THE MOOD by Robbi Sommers. 160 pp. The queen of
erotic tension!   ISBN 1-56280-172-4   11.95

SWIMMING CAT COVE by Lauren Douglas. 192 pp. 2nd
Allison O'Neil Mystery.   ISBN 1-56280-168-6   11.95

THE LOVING LESBIAN by Claire McNab and Sharon Gedan.
240 pp. Explore the experiences that make lesbian love unique.
                                                 ISBN 1-56280-169-4   14.95

COURTED by Celia Cohen. 160 pp. Sparkling romantic
encounter.   ISBN 1-56280-166-X   11.95

SEASONS OF THE HEART by Jackie Calhoun. 240 pp. Romance
through the years.   ISBN 1-56280-167-8   11.95

K. C. BOMBER by Janet McClellan. 208 pp. 1st Tru North
mystery.   ISBN 1-56280-157-0   11.95

LAST RITES by Tracey Richardson. 192 pp. 1st Stevie Houston
mystery.   ISBN 1-56280-164-3   11.95

EMBRACE IN MOTION by Karin Kallmaker. 256 pp. A whirlwind
love affair.   ISBN 1-56280-165-1   11.95

HOT CHECK by Peggy J. Herring. 192 pp. Will workaholic Alice
fall for guitarist Ricky?   ISBN 1-56280-163-5   11.95

OLD TIES by Saxon Bennett. 176 pp. Can Cleo surrender to a
passionate new love? ISBN 1-56280-159-7 11.95

LOVE ON THE LINE by Laura DeHart Young. 176 pp. Will Stef
win Kay's heart? ISBN 1-56280-162-7 11.95

DEVIL'S LEG CROSSING by Kaye Davis. 192 pp. 1st Maris Middleton
mystery. ISBN 1-56280-158-9 11.95

COSTA BRAVA by Marta Balletbo Coll. 144 pp. Read the book,
see the movie! ISBN 1-56280-153-8 11.95

MEETING MAGDALENE & OTHER STORIES by
Marilyn Freeman. 144 pp. Read the book, see the movie!
ISBN 1-56280-170-8 11.95

SECOND FIDDLE by Kate Calloway. 208 pp. P.I. Cassidy James'
second case. ISBN 1-56280-169-6 11.95

LAUREL by Isabel Miller. 128 pp. By the author of the beloved
Patience and Sarah. ISBN 1-56280-146-5 10.95

LOVE OR MONEY by Jackie Calhoun. 240 pp. The romance of
real life. ISBN 1-56280-147-3 10.95

SMOKE AND MIRRORS by Pat Welch. 224 pp. 5th Helen Black
Mystery. ISBN 1-56280-143-0 10.95

DANCING IN THE DARK edited by Barbara Grier & Christine
Cassidy. 272 pp. Erotic love stories by Naiad Press authors.
ISBN 1-56280-144-9 14.95

TIME AND TIME AGAIN by Catherine Ennis. 176 pp. Passionate
love affair. ISBN 1-56280-145-7 10.95

PAXTON COURT by Diane Salvatore. 256 pp. Erotic and wickedly
funny contemporary tale about the business of learning to live
together. ISBN 1-56280-114-7 10.95

INNER CIRCLE by Claire McNab. 208 pp. 8th Carol Ashton
Mystery. ISBN 1-56280-135-X 11.95

LESBIAN SEX: AN ORAL HISTORY by Susan Johnson.
240 pp. Need we say more? ISBN 1-56280-142-2 14.95

WILD THINGS by Karin Kallmaker. 240 pp. By the undisputed
mistress of lesbian romance. ISBN 1-56280-139-2 11.95

THE GIRL NEXT DOOR by Mindy Kaplan. 208 pp. Just what
you'd expect. ISBN 1-56280-140-6 11.95

NOW AND THEN by Penny Hayes. 240 pp. Romance on the
westward journey. ISBN 1-56280-121-X 11.95

HEART ON FIRE by Diana Simmonds. 176 pp. The romantic and
erotic rival of *Curious Wine.* ISBN 1-56280-152-X 11.95

DEATH AT LAVENDER BAY by Lauren Wright Douglas. 208 pp.
1st Allison O'Neil Mystery. ISBN 1-56280-085-X 11.95

YES I SAID YES I WILL by Judith McDaniel. 272 pp. Hot
romance by famous author. ISBN 1-56280-138-4   11.95

FORBIDDEN FIRES by Margaret C. Anderson. Edited by Mathilda
Hills. 176 pp. Famous author's "unpublished" Lesbian romance.
ISBN 1-56280-123-6   21.95

SIDE TRACKS by Teresa Stores. 160 pp. Gender-bending
Lesbians on the road. ISBN 1-56280-122-8   10.95

HOODED MURDER by Annette Van Dyke. 176 pp. 1st Jessie
Batelle Mystery. ISBN 1-56280-134-1   10.95

WILDWOOD FLOWERS by Julia Watts. 208 pp. Hilarious and
heart-warming tale of true love. ISBN 1-56280-127-9   10.95

NEVER SAY NEVER by Linda Hill. 224 pp. Rule #1: Never get involved
with . . . ISBN 1-56280-126-0   10.95

THE SEARCH by Melanie McAllester. 240 pp. Exciting top cop
Tenny Mendoza case. ISBN 1-56280-150-3   10.95

THE WISH LIST by Saxon Bennett. 192 pp. Romance through
the years. ISBN 1-56280-125-2   10.95

FIRST IMPRESSIONS by Kate Calloway. 208 pp. P.I. Cassidy
James' first case. ISBN 1-56280-133-3   10.95

OUT OF THE NIGHT by Kris Bruyer. 192 pp. Spine-tingling
thriller. ISBN 1-56280-120-1   10.95

NORTHERN BLUE by Tracey Richardson. 224 pp. Police recruits
Miki & Miranda — passion in the line of fire. ISBN 1-56280-118-X   10.95

LOVE'S HARVEST by Peggy J. Herring. 176 pp. by the author of
Once More With Feeling. ISBN 1-56280-117-1   10.95

THE COLOR OF WINTER by Lisa Shapiro. 208 pp. Romantic
love beyond your wildest dreams. ISBN 1-56280-116-3   10.95

FAMILY SECRETS by Laura DeHart Young. 208 pp. Enthralling
romance and suspense. ISBN 1-56280-119-8   10.95

INLAND PASSAGE by Jane Rule. 288 pp. Tales exploring conven-
tional & unconventional relationships. ISBN 0-930044-56-8   10.95

DOUBLE BLUFF by Claire McNab. 208 pp. 7th Carol Ashton
Mystery. ISBN 1-56280-096-5   10.95

BAR GIRLS by Lauran Hoffman. 176 pp. See the movie, read
the book! ISBN 1-56280-115-5   10.95

THE FIRST TIME EVER edited by Barbara Grier & Christine
Cassidy. 272 pp. Love stories by Naiad Press authors.
ISBN 1-56280-086-8   14.95

MISS PETTIBONE AND MISS McGRAW by Brenda Weathers.
208 pp. A charming ghostly love story. ISBN 1-56280-151-1   10.95

CHANGES by Jackie Calhoun. 208 pp. Involved romance and
relationships. ISBN 1-56280-083-3   10.95

FAIR PLAY by Rose Beecham. 256 pp. 3rd Amanda Valentine
Mystery. ISBN 1-56280-081-7   10.95

PAYBACK by Celia Cohen. 176 pp. A gripping thriller of romance,
revenge and betrayal. ISBN 1-56280-084-1   10.95

THE BEACH AFFAIR by Barbara Johnson. 224 pp. Sizzling
summer romance/mystery/intrigue. ISBN 1-56280-090-6   10.95

GETTING THERE by Robbi Sommers. 192 pp. Nobody does it
like Robbi! ISBN 1-56280-099-X   10.95

FINAL CUT by Lisa Haddock. 208 pp. 2nd Carmen Ramirez
Mystery. ISBN 1-56280-088-4   10.95

FLASHPOINT by Katherine V. Forrest. 256 pp. A Lesbian
blockbuster! ISBN 1-56280-079-5   10.95

CLAIRE OF THE MOON by Nicole Conn. Audio Book —Read
by Marianne Hyatt. ISBN 1-56280-113-9   16.95

FOR LOVE AND FOR LIFE: INTIMATE PORTRAITS OF
LESBIAN COUPLES by Susan Johnson. 224 pp.
ISBN 1-56280-091-4   14.95

DEVOTION by Mindy Kaplan. 192 pp. See the movie — read
the book! ISBN 1-56280-093-0   10.95

SOMEONE TO WATCH by Jaye Maiman. 272 pp. 4th Robin
Miller Mystery. ISBN 1-56280-095-7   10.95

GREENER THAN GRASS by Jennifer Fulton. 208 pp. A young
woman — a stranger in her bed. ISBN 1-56280-092-2   10.95

TRAVELS WITH DIANA HUNTER by Regine Sands. Erotic
lesbian romp. Audio Book (2 cassettes) ISBN 1-56280-107-4   16.95

CABIN FEVER by Carol Schmidt. 256 pp. Sizzling suspense
and passion. ISBN 1-56280-089-1   10.95

THERE WILL BE NO GOODBYES by Laura DeHart Young. 192
pp. Romantic love, strength, and friendship. ISBN 1-56280-103-1   10.95

FAULTLINE by Sheila Ortiz Taylor. 144 pp. Joyous comic
lesbian novel. ISBN 1-56280-108-2   9.95

OPEN HOUSE by Pat Welch. 176 pp. 4th Helen Black Mystery.
ISBN 1-56280-102-3   10.95

ONCE MORE WITH FEELING by Peggy J. Herring. 240 pp.
Lighthearted, loving romantic adventure. ISBN 1-56280-089-2   10.95

FOREVER by Evelyn Kennedy. 224 pp. Passionate romance — love
overcoming all obstacles. ISBN 1-56280-094-9   10.95

WHISPERS by Kris Bruyer. 176 pp. Romantic ghost story
ISBN 1-56280-082-5   10.95

NIGHT SONGS by Penny Mickelbury. 224 pp. 2nd Gianna Maglione
Mystery. ISBN 1-56280-097-3   10.95

GETTING TO THE POINT by Teresa Stores. 256 pp. Classic
southern Lesbian novel. ISBN 1-56280-100-7 10.95

PAINTED MOON by Karin Kallmaker. 224 pp. Delicious
Kallmaker romance. ISBN 1-56280-075-2 11.95

THE MYSTERIOUS NAIAD edited by Katherine V. Forrest &
Barbara Grier. 320 pp. Love stories by Naiad Press authors.
ISBN 1-56280-074-4 14.95

DAUGHTERS OF A CORAL DAWN by Katherine V. Forrest.
240 pp. Tenth Anniversay Edition. ISBN 1-56280-104-X 11.95

BODY GUARD by Claire McNab. 208 pp. 6th Carol Ashton
Mystery. ISBN 1-56280-073-6 11.95

CACTUS LOVE by Lee Lynch. 192 pp. Stories by the beloved
storyteller. ISBN 1-56280-071-X 9.95

SECOND GUESS by Rose Beecham. 216 pp. 2nd Amanda Valentine
Mystery. ISBN 1-56280-069-8 9.95

A RAGE OF MAIDENS by Lauren Wright Douglas. 240 pp. 6th Caitlin
Reece Mystery. ISBN 1-56280-068-X 10.95

TRIPLE EXPOSURE by Jackie Calhoun. 224 pp. Romantic drama
involving many characters. ISBN 1-56280-067-1 10.95

UP, UP AND AWAY by Catherine Ennis. 192 pp. Delightful
romance. ISBN 1-56280-065-5 11.95

PERSONAL ADS by Robbi Sommers. 176 pp. Sizzling short
stories. ISBN 1-56280-059-0 11.95

CROSSWORDS by Penny Sumner. 256 pp. 2nd Victoria Cross
Mystery. ISBN 1-56280-064-7 9.95

SWEET CHERRY WINE by Carol Schmidt. 224 pp. A novel of
suspense. ISBN 1-56280-063-9 9.95

CERTAIN SMILES by Dorothy Tell. 160 pp. Erotic short stories.
ISBN 1-56280-066-3 9.95

EDITED OUT by Lisa Haddock. 224 pp. 1st Carmen Ramirez
Mystery. ISBN 1-56280-077-9 9.95

WEDNESDAY NIGHTS by Camarin Grae. 288 pp. Sexy
adventure. ISBN 1-56280-060-4 10.95

SMOKEY O by Celia Cohen. 176 pp. Relationships on the
playing field. ISBN 1-56280-057-4 9.95

KATHLEEN O'DONALD by Penny Hayes. 256 pp. Rose and
Kathleen find each other and employment in 1909 NYC.
ISBN 1-56280-070-1 9.95

STAYING HOME by Elisabeth Nonas. 256 pp. Molly and Alix
want a baby . . . or do they? ISBN 1-56280-076-0 10.95

TRUE LOVE by Jennifer Fulton. 240 pp. Six lesbians searching
for love in all the "right" places. ISBN 1-56280-035-3 10.95

KEEPING SECRETS by Penny Mickelbury. 208 pp. 1st Gianna
Maglione Mystery. ISBN 1-56280-052-3 9.95

THE ROMANTIC NAIAD edited by Katherine V. Forrest &
Barbara Grier. 336 pp. Love stories by Naiad Press authors.
ISBN 1-56280-054-X 14.95

UNDER MY SKIN by Jaye Maiman. 336 pp. 3rd Robin Miller
Mystery. ISBN 1-56280-049-3. 10.95

CAR POOL by Karin Kallmaker. 272pp. Lesbians on wheels
and then some! ISBN 1-56280-048-5 10.95

NOT TELLING MOTHER: STORIES FROM A LIFE by Diane
Salvatore. 176 pp. Her 3rd novel. ISBN 1-56280-044-2 9.95

GOBLIN MARKET by Lauren Wright Douglas. 240pp. 5th Caitlin
Reece Mystery. ISBN 1-56280-047-7 10.95

LONG GOODBYES by Nikki Baker. 256 pp. 3rd Virginia Kelly
Mystery. ISBN 1-56280-042-6 9.95

FRIENDS AND LOVERS by Jackie Calhoun. 224 pp. Mid-
western Lesbian lives and loves. ISBN 1-56280-041-8 11.95

BEHIND CLOSED DOORS by Robbi Sommers. 192 pp. Hot,
erotic short stories. ISBN 1-56280-039-6 11.95

CLAIRE OF THE MOON by Nicole Conn. 192 pp. See the
movie — read the book! ISBN 1-56280-038-8 10.95

SILENT HEART by Claire McNab. 192 pp. Exotic Lesbian
romance. ISBN 1-56280-036-1 10.95

THE SPY IN QUESTION by Amanda Kyle Williams. 256 pp.
4th Madison McGuire Mystery. ISBN 1-56280-037-X 9.95

SAVING GRACE by Jennifer Fulton. 240 pp. Adventure and
romantic entanglement. ISBN 1-56280-051-5 10.95

CURIOUS WINE by Katherine V. Forrest. 176 pp. Tenth Anniver-
sary Edition. The most popular contemporary Lesbian love story.
ISBN 1-56280-053-1 11.95
Audio Book (2 cassettes) ISBN 1-56280-105-8 16.95

CHAUTAUQUA by Catherine Ennis. 192 pp. Exciting, romantic
adventure. ISBN 1-56280-032-9 9.95

A PROPER BURIAL by Pat Welch. 192 pp. 3rd Helen Black
Mystery. ISBN 1-56280-033-7 9.95

SILVERLAKE HEAT: A Novel of Suspense by Carol Schmidt.
240 pp. Rhonda is as hot as Laney's dreams. ISBN 1-56280-031-0 9.95

LOVE, ZENA BETH by Diane Salvatore. 224 pp. The most talked
about lesbian novel of the nineties! ISBN 1-56280-030-2 10.95

A DOORYARD FULL OF FLOWERS by Isabel Miller. 160 pp.
Stories incl. 2 sequels to *Patience and Sarah.* ISBN 1-56280-029-9 9.95

MURDER BY TRADITION by Katherine V. Forrest. 288 pp. 4th
Kate Delafield Mystery.   ISBN 1-56280-002-7   11.95

THE EROTIC NAIAD edited by Katherine V. Forrest & Barbara
Grier. 224 pp. Love stories by Naiad Press authors.
                                           ISBN 1-56280-026-4   14.95

DEAD CERTAIN by Claire McNab. 224 pp. 5th Carol Ashton
Mystery.   ISBN 1-56280-027-2   9.95

CRAZY FOR LOVING by Jaye Maiman. 320 pp. 2nd Robin Miller
Mystery.   ISBN 1-56280-025-6   10.95

STONEHURST by Barbara Johnson. 176 pp. Passionate regency
romance.   ISBN 1-56280-024-8   9.95

INTRODUCING AMANDA VALENTINE by Rose Beecham.
256 pp. 1st Amanda Valentine Mystery.   ISBN 1-56280-021-3   10.95

UNCERTAIN COMPANIONS by Robbi Sommers. 204 pp.
Steamy, erotic novel.   ISBN 1-56280-017-5   11.95

A TIGER'S HEART by Lauren W. Douglas. 240 pp. 4th Caitlin
Reece Mystery.   ISBN 1-56280-018-3   9.95

PAPERBACK ROMANCE by Karin Kallmaker. 256 pp. A
delicious romance.   ISBN 1-56280-019-1   10.95

THE LAVENDER HOUSE MURDER by Nikki Baker. 224 pp.
2nd Virginia Kelly Mystery.   ISBN 1-56280-012-4   9.95

PASSION BAY by Jennifer Fulton. 224 pp. Passionate romance,
virgin beaches, tropical skies.   ISBN 1-56280-028-0   10.95

STICKS AND STONES by Jackie Calhoun. 208 pp. Contemporary
lesbian lives and loves.   ISBN 1-56280-020-5   9.95
Audio Book (2 cassettes)   ISBN 1-56280-106-6   16.95

UNDER THE SOUTHERN CROSS by Claire McNab. 192 pp.
Romantic nights Down Under.   ISBN 1-56280-011-6   11.95

GRASSY FLATS by Penny Hayes. 256 pp. Lesbian romance in
the '30s.   ISBN 1-56280-010-8   9.95

A SINGULAR SPY by Amanda K. Williams. 192 pp. 3rd
Madison McGuire Mystery.   ISBN 1-56280-008-6   8.95

THE END OF APRIL by Penny Sumner. 240 pp. 1st Victoria
Cross Mystery.   ISBN 1-56280-007-8   8.95

KISS AND TELL by Robbi Sommers. 192 pp. Scorching stories
by the author of *Pleasures.*   ISBN 1-56280-005-1   11.95

These are just a few of the many Naiad Press titles — we are the oldest and
largest lesbian/feminist publishing company in the world. We also offer an
enormous selection of lesbian video products. Please request a complete
catalog. We offer personal service; we encourage and welcome direct mail
orders from individuals who have limited access to bookstores carrying our
publications.